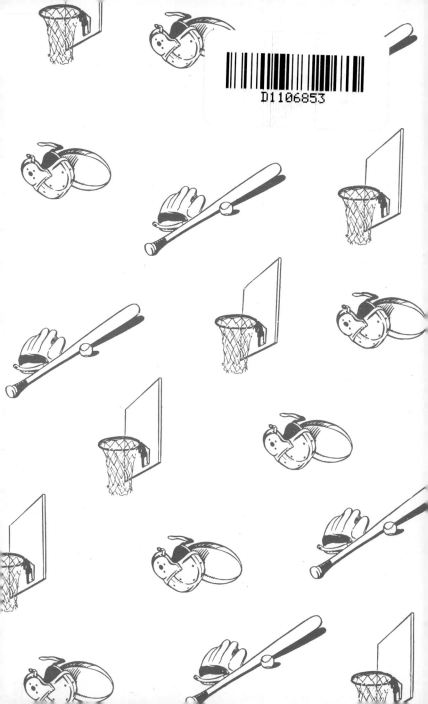

D1106853

Joey DiPol

Dugout Jinx

"If you can get the signs, Colin, the Mules can too,"
Kildare said in a low voice.

"If you can get the signs, Chip, the Mules can too,"
Kildane said in a low voice.

A CHIP HILTON SPORTS STORY

Dugout Jinx

BY CLAIR BEE

GROSSET & DUNLAP   Publishers   New York

PRINTED IN THE UNITED STATES OF AMERICA

TO

HAROLD UPLINGER

Student, Athlete, Friend

Contents

Contents

Dugout Jinx

CHAPTER 1

WHAT PRICE GLORY

PARKVILLE baseball fans are pretty much like other fans the country over. If anything, they go a little further. They are loyal to the home-town team—first, last, and all the time—win, lose, or draw. In addition, they believe aggressive Eddie Duer, balding, eagle-beaked leader of the Parkville Bears, is the craftiest manager in the game and miles ahead of his contemporary diamond impresarios. All of which partly explains why Duer's latest brain storm was creating such a furore in the fanatical baseball city of Parkville. And why Bear Stadium was jammed with fans that Tuesday morning, despite the fact that the Bears were not practicing and were not scheduled to play until the following Thursday night.

Parkville's fans were there to get a look-see at the current year's high school stars from eight different states who had been chosen to compete on their respective teams in Duer's brand-new promotion, "The World's Greatest Amateur All-Star Tournament." One hundred and twenty youngsters, some already registered in college and looking forward to four more years of study and baseball, and some on a last vacation be-

1

fore going to work in the business field or entering a trade. Whatever their plans, naturally every boy in the tournament was eager to gain recognition as a prospect for big-league baseball. And every one of them was determined to prove that his team was the best in the tournament.

There were a number of unfamiliar faces in Bear Stadium that morning, too. They included well-dressed men who were obviously baseball enthusiasts. And when the fans sized them up, noted their keen eyes, tanned faces, and well-set-up physiques, they wondered why these unknown professionals were so far from the scene of the close race between the Yankees and the Red Sox in the American League and the "down-the-stretch" dogfight between the Giants and Cards in the National League. These sun-browned strangers looked like baseball experts! And they were!

Every big-league chain was represented in the group of eagle-eyed scouts who were watching the agile youngsters working out on the sun-baked diamond. There were a few bird dogs in the stands, too. Men who scouted "on their own," but who had an agreement with a scout or a big-league chain whereby likely prospects were signed up with the understanding that there would be a bonus for every player they recommended who made the grade in the minors, and a big bonus if the player made good and "went up" to the big time.

The team which was working out that Tuesday morning was only one of the eight teams which the talent detectives meant to watch. These experts were in a baseball scout's heaven. Where else could one see a hundred or more hand-picked baseball prospects from eight different states in three short days? Who could say that a fellow might not discover another Babe Ruth, Joe DiMaggio, Stan Musial, or Bob Feller, before the week ended? Not the finished product, of course, not the King of Swat, the Joltin' Joe, Stan the Man, or Rapid Robert, but the diamond in the rough. These talent detectives were qualified through years of playing, managing, and scouting experience to recognize the future "greats" of baseball.

Stu Gardner, veteran scout for the Drakes, probably was one of the few chain representatives on hand who knew most of the players on the field at that particular moment. Gardner had spent several weeks watching and waiting for two of the kids batting and throwing down below to be graduated from high school. His eyes shifted from the tall, blond boy who was leisurely warming up in the pitcher's box in front of the third-base dugout to the bulky first baseman who was taking part in the infield practice. His thoughts were interrupted by the fan sitting on his right.

"I figure you're a scout," the man ventured. "That right?"

Gardner smiled. "That's right," he said, without taking his eyes off the scene below.

"Who do you like out there?" the fan asked.

"That's easy," Gardner said quietly. "I like the two kids from Valley Falls, the chucker warming up in front of the dugout and the big lefty first baseman."

"You ever see them before?" the man on Gardner's left queried.

Gardner smiled ruefully and nodded his head. "I sure did," he said. "Why, I shadowed those two kids for two months while they were in high school, just waiting for them to graduate so I could offer them a contract."

"What did graduating from high school have to do with it?"

"Well," Gardner explained patiently, "our chain plays the game according to the rules. According to the rules and according to ethics," he added. "You see, my boss, the general manager of the Drakes, believes that a high school boy should not be approached until he has earned his high school diploma. Far as that's concerned, he never feels too bad when a kid says he wants to wait till after he's been graduated from college. So we keep tabs on them and contact them all the way through college, till the boy gets his sheepskin. But we better not lose the kid then!"

"What happened after those two kids out there graduated from high school?"

"Nothing! They want to go to college. And a boy who signs a contract automatically becomes a professional and that eliminates him from college ball."

"Couldn't you sign them, anyway? I mean, can't a boy sign up and go to college and keep his mouth shut and play college ball just the same?"

"Well, I guess he can if he's that kind of kid," Gardner said slowly, "and if the scout who signs him is that kind of character."

"I say a kid ought to get all he can get while he can get it!" someone behind Gardner asserted loudly.

Gardner turned his head to face the speaker. "Some kids just aren't like that," he said softly. "Some kids have ambitions and dreams and hopes, and money is only incidental in their desire to accomplish their goal. Now you take that kid warming up. Why, he could have gotten, can still get so far as that's concerned, a bonus of ten or twenty thousand just to sign to play after he gets through college."

"He must be nuts!" the fan in the back said loudly.

"Or rich!" someone added.

"No," Gardner continued, "he's not rich by a long shot, far from it. In fact, he's hard up, had to work his way through high school, and his heart is set on following in the footsteps of his dad, set on playing college ball and getting an education."

"I still think he's nuts," the fan behind Gardner insisted. "Why, I know a lot of college graduates who can't make twenty thousand dollars in *five* years."

"What price glory!" someone said dryly.

"Money isn't everything, you know," Gardner said quietly. "Baseball's my business and I'd give my right arm to sign that kid out there to a contract. But if he were my son I'd be awfully proud of the stand he's taken. Some kids aren't for sale. They value their dreams and ambitions far more than money. He's that kind of kid."

"You know any of those other kids out there? Any other Plainsmen?"

Gardner shifted his eyes from position to position before answering. "Yes," he said, nodding his head, "I know most of them. That is, those who seem to be better prepared for professional baseball. You see, I scouted the state high school tournament when these kids were chosen to represent the Plainsmen. That boy catching Hilton is from Valley Falls, too. Name is Smith, Soapy Smith. He's a fair catcher but not in a class with Hilton or Cohen. Cohen's the first baseman."

"You sure seem high on the chucker. Wha'd you say his name was?"

"Hilton, Chip Hilton. He's the best big-league prospect I ever saw and I've seen a lot of them."

"He must be something!"

Gardner smiled grimly. "You'll see," he said confidently. "That is, if you're here tomorrow night. The Plainsmen play the Rebels according to my schedule."

"Look, Mister," the fan said proudly, "I'll be here *every* game. The folks in this man's town go whole hog where baseball's concerned. Why, every ticket for the series was sold the first three days they went on sale. Eddie Duer's a smart manager and he's a smart promoter, too."

"Only thing is," someone added, "we're afraid one of the big-league teams will sign him up. He's another John McGraw!"

"How about some of those other kids out there? Any of them as good as that Chip Hilton? I mean, in their own positions?"

Gardner shook his head and scanned the field reflectively. "No," he said firmly, "none of the kids out there are in Hilton's class. The first baseman is about the best, next to the chucker." He gestured toward the field. "That's a great aggregation of kids, though, and I could be wrong about some of them, especially the outfielders. That team will be playing in the final game come Saturday afternoon or I don't know baseball! Guess I'll grab me a sandwich. See you fellows later."

Gardner wasn't hungry but he wanted to get away from the quizzing. He liked the friendly fans but he had work to do. Besides, the discussion had led his thoughts to his first meeting with Chip Hilton and Henry Rockwell, the kid's high school coach. Stu bought a sandwich and a bottle of coke and stood just behind the last row of seats, looking down on the field and thinking about the tall, stringy chucker who had been the subject of most of the conversation.

Stu Gardner knew Chip Hilton, all right. Stu guessed he knew the kid almost as well as if the chucker had been his own son. He had watched the boy fight back after experiencing an ordeal which would have taxed the courage of anyone; had seen the kid outwit several scoundrels who had tried to use him in their plans to ensnare the boy's coach.

For the next ten minutes Gardner lived through those three hectic days he had spent at State University when Chip Hilton had pitched his team to a great opening-round victory only to become the victim of a last-minute plot. A plot which was diabolic in its construction and execution, and which did, in fact, partly succeed; would have succeeded entirely if the kid hadn't been a fighter, a boy who didn't know when he was whipped.

Hilton had been framed by a cheap hoodlum, who had used an innocent autograph on a bogus baseball contract to keep the star hurler from pitching the championship game. The state eligibility committee had declared Hilton ineligible the morning of the contest, and the fiendish plan would have succeeded if the boy himself had not exposed the plotters a few hours later. Gardner was in on the finish of that deal; in on it at the very moment when, only by chance, Chip had recognized the one person in the world who could have been the instigator of the hoax. Stu had been in the car which chased the scoundrel and had been in on the fight and the capture of one of the plotters. Then he'd seen Chip pitch the last nine innings of a nineteen-inning game, only to lose the pitchers' duel when a teammate misjudged an easy fly, and a foul ball had hit a pebble and rolled into fair territory scoring the runner. It had been a tough loss for the youngster, but he had taken it like a champion.

"And that's what he is," Gardner murmured aloud, "a champ!"

Gardner had been deep in thought but, subconsciously, he had been aware of a familiar voice. Then he heard the voice again and recognized the owner before he located his position. It didn't take long to find the speaker. He was talking loudly to a group of surrounding fans who seemed to be getting a big kick out of the conversation.

"Ho–hum," Stu Gardner sighed. "Here's trouble!"

He studied the shrewd, pasty face of the man. "Gabby Breen," he whispered. "He *would* show up!"

Gabby Breen was a much-publicized talent scout. A shrewd, hustling, fast-talking bird dog with absolutely no scruples in his dealings with anyone. The tall, stoop-shouldered man was dressed in flashy clothes, and his free and breezy manner, his loud voice, and his garrulity attracted attention everywhere. Given a few minutes in any group, he could advertise himself so well that every person within earshot soon knew he was a baseball scout and a talent promoter.

Early in the summer Breen had joined the scouting staff of the Mules and had rapidly wormed himself into the confidence of Boots Rines, their manager. He had managed to attract the attention of the owner of the Hedgetown club, H. B. "Hoot" Kearns, and had used his talents to ingratiate himself into the good graces of that worried baseball mogul.

The Mules, Hedgetown's pride, had won the pennant the previous year, and, despite the advice of Kearns, Boots Rines had elected to stick with his championship club for the current year. However, the Parkville Bears had strengthened their team with several youngsters that Breen had urged Rines to sign and, more important, had taken the league lead early in the season and held it all the way. It was easy to understand why the relations between Kearns and Rines were strained. Breen hadn't helped the situation, despite his apparent friendship for Rines. The wily scout had his eye on the manager's job and insidiously was working toward that objective.

"You Parkvillagers got yourselves a pretty fair country ball club," Breen continued loudly, "but you'll never win the pennant!"

"Why not?" someone demanded. "Shucks, we're out in front and got only the Mules to beat."

"Mules will take all ten of those games," Breen retorted, "easy!"

"Not with Scissors chuckin'," a fan yelled. "You watch him cut the Mules down Thursday night!"

"Aw, Kildane's just a Boy Scout," Breen said disdainfully. "He ain't got nothin' but a glove and a prayer!"

"All he did was beat the Mules five out of seven!"

Breen's face flushed, but the burst of anger passed quickly and when he spoke there was no trace of antagonism in his voice. "Aw, Boots Rines gave you them games, used his weak sisters on the hill every time."

"I s'pose Lefty Turner's a weak sister!"

Breen laughed boisterously. "Turner? Shucks, he was takin' it easy." He gestured toward the field. "Say, you mean to say you Parkville fans are fallin' for this little-boy stuff? Duer got everyone in this burg hypnotized? What's this all about?"

"You know what it's all about," someone chided good-naturedly. "You know, or you wouldn't be here. Guess Rines is gettin' worried. Musta sent you over here to do a little spyin'."

Breen laughed. But this time it was a strained, forced laugh. "Aw, Boots ain't interested in this kid stuff. All he's interested in is winnin' the pennant. But that don't go for me! I like to pick up kids and develop 'em into big-league prospects. Why, I got me 'bout thirty kids signed up right now, and about half of them are big-show stuff, sure's shootin'!"

"Any in this league?"

"Sure, lots of them! You got one of them playin' right

here in Parkville. The best keystone operator in the business!"

"You mean Corky Squill?"

"No one else! I signed him for Duer before I tied up with the Mules."

"He's good all right," a fan acknowledged grudgingly, "if you go for that kind of ballplayer."

The man behind Breen tapped him on the shoulder. "If you're lookin' for a first sacker you don't have to look any further than that kid out there right now," he said. "Watch him!"

"Strange as it may seem," Breen said loudly, "that's exactly what I'm lookin' for"—he gestured toward first base—"that big southpaw the one you mean?"

"Yeah, watch him now. Watch him throw."

Breen grunted. "Huh, the kid's got an arm, all right, but first sackers gotta be hitters, too."

"He can hit! See that house stickin' up beyond the right-field fence? Well, that house is across the street and he bounced two, three of 'em, off the roof a little while ago."

"Means nothin'," Breen said lightly, with an exaggerated gesture. "See if he does it in the game."

Back of this oddly assorted group, Stu Gardner was seething. He knew Gabby Breen to be a faker, a fellow who cared nothing about young kids except to exploit them to the fullest extent. And Gardner knew all about the tricks Breen used to impress youngsters. The man had exploited every boy who had been unfortunate enough to believe in the wily schemer's promises. Stu wished baseball could do something about fellows like Gabby Breen. Breen was trouble for young kids with big-league ambitions. Trouble with a capital T. What sort of mess was he cooking up in that devious mind of his now?

CHAPTER 2

TELEVISION ALL-STAR

WILLIAM "CHIP" HILTON would have been greatly embarrassed had he known anyone in the ball park was talking about his particular baseball prowess when there were so many other outstanding ballplayers on the scene. Right now, Chip felt so right, so perfectly relaxed, that he wasn't thinking about anything except his pitching. He was basking in that zestful feeling which comes to a chucker who is right. Chip's fast one was hopping and his slider was twisting a mile. But he didn't throw himself away. He knew when to apply the brakes, and he was pacing himself and willing to call it a day when Pat Reynolds, coach of the Plainsmen, called, "That's it, gang! Hit the showers!"

Chip put on his sweater and started for the grandstand, but Reynolds checked him. "Come here a second, Chip," he said, beckoning with his finger. "I want you to meet someone you ought to know."

Chip glanced at the young stranger who had joined Reynolds in front of the dugout. The man was tall, almost skinny, and his height dwarfed Chip's six-feet-two. Chip figured the man was a good six-six. "Must be a basketball player," he speculated to himself. "He's

11

sure tall enough." His interest quickened. "Maybe he's a big-time pro."

"Chip," Reynolds said proudly, "I want you to meet Scissors Kildane. I guess you've heard of him."

Chip nodded eagerly and extended his hand. He'd heard of Scissors Kildane, all right! Who hadn't? Kildane was the rookie sensation of the Midwestern League, already tabbed for the big leagues and regarded as the greatest pitching "find" since Bob Feller. Kildane's long fingers twined around Chip's hand like steel bands as the big chucker pumped his arm and smiled down at him with friendly, gray-green eyes.

"Hiya, feller," Scissors greeted him heartily. "I've heard of you, too! Pat's been talking about you all morning. Says you're the best pitcher in the tournament."

Chip reddened and shifted his weight. He was angry with himself for being embarrassed. He tried to say something, anything, but the words wouldn't come. Reynolds saved the day.

"Scissors wants you to appear on his television program tonight, Chip, and I told him you'd be tickled to death."

Chip wasn't tickled to death, but he wasn't able to say anything, so he just nodded his head and smiled and then suddenly the words came.

"I—I don't think I'd be any good on a television program, Mr. Kildane."

"The name's Scissors," Kildane said lightly, "if you don't mind. And you'll be all right, leave that to me. Suppose I pick you up at the hotel at, say, seven-fifteen. Okay?"

"Okay," Chip agreed lamely, "okay."

Later that afternoon, in the bleachers, Chip mentally kicked himself for being so agreeable. At the dinner table that evening with Biggie and Soapy he fidgeted and fussed until his pals became suspicious and pried the secret from his unwilling lips.

"With Scissors Kildane!" Soapy blurted. "Oh, boy, me for that! Let's go!"

That was why Kildane had three passengers in his car a few minutes later when he pulled away from the Park Hotel and headed for the television studio. None of the three boys had ever been on a television program and they were bewildered by the confusion of the cluttered scene when they arrived on the set. But Scissors Kildane appeared to be right at home, and Chip wished he could feel as little concerned as the easy-mannered pitching star.

"You fellows sit down over here on these chairs," Scissors directed. "I've got to get some Florida suntan, they call it pancake make-up, on this physiog of mine. Won't be a second."

There were three or four sets in the room, and Chip's eyes filled with amazement as he watched the man-manipulated cameras moving forward and back as they went through the rehearsals for the programs which were to follow. One set in a corner of the big room displayed a modern, up-to-date kitchen. The members of the cast were on the set, ready to go as soon as Kildane's program was finished. In another corner a vaudeville show was being rehearsed.

"Gosh," Soapy whispered, "it's like seeing four movies at once."

In a few minutes Scissors was back, accompanied by a youngster about Chip's age. Kildane led the boy directly to Chip. "Chip," he said, "I want you to meet Johnny Gordon. Johnny, this is Chip Hilton. You fellows better get acquainted. You're pitching against one another tomorrow night."

Johnny Gordon was about Chip's height and almost the same weight. The two boys shook hands and smiled. Chip then introduced Gordon to his two buddies. "This is Soapy Smith, Johnny. He's our catcher," Chip explained. "Biggie, here, plays first base."

Gordon shook hands with Soapy and Biggie and they stood there, awkwardly shifting from one foot to the other. Kildane broke the silence. "Chip, from what I hear, the Plainsmen and the Rebels are pretty evenly matched. It ought to be a good game. How do you fellows think you'll make out?"

Soapy startled everyone by snorting loudly. "We'll kill 'em," he said aggressively, "kill 'em dead!"

There was a shocked silence until Biggie balled a big fist and punched the exuberant Soapy on the shoulder. Soapy's protestations and Chip's chuckle eased the situation.

"No one pays any attention to the Valley Falls moron, Johnny," Chip said lightly. "He's just trying to get into the act."

But Soapy didn't take Chip's remark at all lightly. "Do you think I could, Mr. Kildane?" the redhead queried, turning his head quickly in the direction of Scissors. "Do you think I could get into the act; get on the show? Boy, if I ever went back home and told them I was on television—"

Scissors had no chance to answer Soapy's question. The director gave Kildane the cue, and before Chip knew it, he was standing beside Johnny Gordon in the background of the set and Scissors Kildane was talking away as if he were in his own home; the dreaded "mike" hanging down from the boom on the big camera didn't seem to bother him at all.

"—You know, fans, this baseball tournament is the brain child of our manager, Eddie Duer, and all of us players who work for and under Eddie think it's the best thing he ever did. It's no secret that Eddie is after some of these kids for his own team and, along with the rest of the Bears, I hope he gets some of them, especially a couple of the pitchers.

"And that brings me to some information I think you ought to have. . . . You know, every coach of these eight tournament teams has been promised that no scout shall be permitted to talk to an All-Star concerning a big-league contract signing until after the kid reaches home—until the respective coach has gotten his team back home. Knowing Eddie as we do, we know he'll stick to that rule himself.

"Just because it's Eddie's idea and because the kids are his guests doesn't mean he won't stick to the rules. I thought you'd like to know that—since there are about a hundred big-league scouts in town.

"And now, sports fans, I want to introduce my special guests."

While Kildane had been talking, Chip's thoughts had wandered. Maybe he'd be a Scissors Kildane someday. . . . Maybe he had made the wrong choice with respect to college. . . . Kildane wasn't more than two or three years older and here he was making a lot of money and in a position to do things for his family. . . . Maybe Chip Hilton ought to forget about college and an education and think more about his mother. . . .

Chip looked up, then, and nearly laughed out loud. Soapy had his thumbs in his ears and was wiggling his fingers and making faces at Kildane. But the freckle face sobered when Kildane caught him. Scissors laughed, too, almost halted in his speech, but managed to go on.

"Fans, on my right you see Johnny Gordon, a south-paw who will start for the Rebel All-Stars tomorrow night. Here on my left is Chip Hilton who will pitch for the Plainsmen. In just a moment I'm coming back to these two boys and we'll ask them some questions about their pitching, and sort of get acquainted. But first, I want to remind you that tomorrow morning, at nine o'clock sharp, the Cornhusker All-Stars meet the Lakers in the opening game of the tournament. Immediately following that game the Miners and Hillbillies tangle and, in the late afternoon, around about four o'clock, I would judge, the Yankees and the Buckeyes square off. Now, let's get back to our guests, the chuckers who are going to start the nightcap game.

"Johnny, have you ever pitched night ball before?"

Gordon seemed right at home. "No, Mr. Kildane," he said calmly, "I've never pitched a night game but I'm anxious to give it a try."

Kildane turned to Chip. "And how about you, Hilton? Chip, have you ever pitched a night game?"

Chip was surprised at his own voice. He was talking, all right, but the words seemed to come from far off, sounded like those of a stranger. "Yes, Mr. Kildane, I've pitched at night, but never in a big-league ball park. It's got me a little worried."

"That's nothing." Scissors laughed. "I get worried, too. Every time I look down the alley and see those big sticks waving around, I get plenty worried. But, you know, chuckers have the edge in night games. It's the hitters who really have to worry. There are lots of shadows, the background is poor, and if a chucker has a lot of fast stuff—or, for example, a lot of tricky stuff—why, you've got a big edge on the hitter. You know, fellows, hitters don't wait 'em out much at night. I figure that's particularly true of high school players and that's why control is so important. Another thing, if your fast stuff is right, use it early and then sort of fall back on your trick stuff later—hooks and sliders and knucklers. You're going to get a lot of fun out of this series, and you're going to like that mound out there and this Parkville crowd. You've never played baseball before a crowd like this one. Gordon, what's your pitching speciality?"

"I'm supposed to have a little bit of speed and control, Mr. Kildane, but I don't have much soft stuff. In fact, my coach said he doesn't think I'll ever learn a change of pace."

Kildane turned to Chip. "Hilton, suppose you tell our televiewers just what you expect to throw against Johnny, here, tomorrow night."

Chip shook his head and smiled. "I'll try to use my fast ball, just as you said, at the start. Then work a little bit on my slider—and, well, I guess I'm like Johnny. My coach, Henry Rockwell, over at Valley Falls, used to tell me my roundhouse was my change-of-pace pitch."

Kildane laughed. "That's me all over," he said. "I throw a hard one and then I throw an easy one and that's my change of pace. Well, let's get away from this pitching—"

"Excuse me, Mr. Kildane," Chip interrupted quickly, "I'd like to see how you hold your knuckler. I've heard Mr. Reynolds talk about your knuckler and I'm working on a blooper pitch—that's what I call it—but I don't know whether I'm holding it right or not."

Kildane nodded his head approvingly. "That's the ticket. That's what our televiewers like. Throw me that ball, Hugh, will you? Now, fellows, here's the ball and I'm going to show you how I hold my knuckler. Keep in mind, though, it doesn't make much difference whether you hold the ball flat against the palm with the fingers and the thumb out straight, or whether you hold it with the thumb and the little finger and then bend the inside fingers down and rest the ball against them. Important thing is to use the same sort of windup and throwing motion. That's where the deception is. You see, it isn't the pitch as much as it is the deception of the windup.

"Now I guess you televiewers can see how I'm holding the ball—with my thumb and little finger, and resting it against the knuckles of my three inside fingers. Of course I try to conceal it as long as possible. All the pitchers try to do that, try to keep the ball hidden from the batter as long as possible and then use the same motion in the windup as they do for their fast ball. Now, that's about enough of pitching. I think we ought to talk a little bit about hitting. I heard Pat Reynolds say that you were a switch hitter, Hilton. Which side do you like best?"

"Well, Mr. Kildane," Chip said awkwardly, "I'm not a very good hitter, but I like to bat from the first-base side of the plate best because I'm that much closer to first, and when I follow through on a hit, it pulls me around in stride and helps me to beat out infield hits."

"From what Pat tells me, you don't hit many on the ground," Kildane chided. "He says you hit a long ball and often! How about you, Johnny? How do you hit?"

"I hit from the third-base side of the plate, Mr. Kildane. It seems funny, perhaps, me being a southpaw, but I never did learn to hit from the other side. In fact, when I do get over on that side I can't even seem to see the ball. I can't focus on the ball, can't seem to hit a lick."

Kildane nodded understandingly. "There might be a reason for that, Johnny. I'm glad you brought it up. You know, folks, every person has what we call a master eye, usually the right eye for lefty hitters and the left eye for righty hitters. Fellows like Chip, here, switch hitters—well, they can focus either eye and that becomes their master eye, according to the side from which they hit. I want you televiewers to try something. I'm going to take the ball and put it right here on this book. Okay? Now, I want you to do just as I say. First, close your right eye, put your hand over it, and focus your left eye on the ball. Got that? Now cover your left eye and focus your right eye on the ball. What happened? The ball moved when you changed from right to left and left to right, didn't it? All right, try it again. Chip, you and Johnny try it, too. I'm going to try it."

Just as Kildane said, the ball seemed to change positions. When Chip closed his left eye the ball jumped to the left and up, and when he closed his right eye the ball jumped to the right and down. He'd never thought of that before. Maybe he could work on the theory and improve his hitting.

"That's fine," Kildane concluded. "Now, Hilton, here's a bat. Move over here in front of this camera and stand just the way you do when you're at the plate. Let's see your stance and how you hold the bat when you're batting from the third-base side of the plate. That's it! Hold it! Now swing right through just as if you were batting. Don't be afraid. Take a full swing."

Chip swung the bat through in a full arc, finishing up with the bat back over his left shoulder.

"Now let's try that on the other side, from the first-base side of the plate. Watch closely, folks, this boy is a fine hitter from either side of the plate, and he seems to have the same form from both sides. Now, Chip, pull the bat through just as you did before. Try to imagine you see the ball coming and you're going to knock it right out of the park, just like you hope to do tomorrow night."

Chip pulled the bat through in a clean level sweep and ended with the bat over his right shoulder. He felt foolish, posing that way, but Kildane ended his embarrassment when he slapped him on the back and took the bat away.

"There you are, folks. Now you know why Chip Hilton is a good hitter. Me? I can't hit a basketball! I swing like a rusty gate!

"Folks, we don't have much time left, but I've got a couple of other boys I want you to meet. Come over here, Smith. You too, Cohen. Folks, this is Soapy Smith. Comes from Valley Falls. Plays with the Plainsmen in the tournament and is a catcher. In fact, he caught Chip Hilton all through high school. Smith, just what does this battery mate of yours throw? He's been a little on the modest side."

"I'll say he has," Soapy chirped. "You know, Mr. Kildane, I never saw you work, but I'll bet you haven't got half the stuff Chip's got!"

Kildane chuckled. "You don't have to tell me that—but you can tell our audience. Tell them—"

"Ladies and gentlemen telesewers—" Soapy began, then stopped and placed his hand over his mouth and looked appealingly at Kildane.

"You mean televiewers," Kildane corrected.

"Er—televiewers, Chip's got a lightning fast ball and he's got a screwball and he's got a blooper and a good change-up curve and he's got a crossfire slider and an underhand twister that I can't even catch. He fools the batters and me too!" Soapy finished with a rush. He had rehearsed what he was going to say, all right, but the mike had mesmerized him, had almost tongue-tied the loquacious clown.

"That repertory would fool most anybody," Kildane

said dryly. He turned to Biggie Cohen. "Cohen, say hello to our televiewers. Folks, Cohen is another Valley Falls boy. He's about six-four, weighs two-thirty, and plays a mean game at first base. You played football, too, didn't you, Cohen?"

Biggie nodded his head. "Yes, Mr. Kildane. I played four years at tackle."

"Pat Reynolds tells me you're a southpaw. Tells me you're an ideal first baseman. A pretty good target for your infielders, I'd say. How do you hit, Cohen? From the left or the right side of the plate?"

"I'm a southpaw hitter, Mr. Kildane. I hit from the first-base side of the plate. I don't know much about that master-eye stuff you've been talking about, but I can't hit a thing from the third-base side of the plate."

"You do pretty well from the first-base side, though. Well, folks, that just about cleans the bases until tomorrow night when I'll have some more of the All-Stars on hand to meet you. So, until then, this is Scissors Kildane saying so long and good luck for Johnny Gordon, Chip Hilton, Soapy Smith, and Biggie Cohen. See you at the stadium!"

Kildane slapped each boy on the shoulder and said, "Nice going! You were great! Come on, I'm going to set 'em up to the sodas. Give me a couple of minutes to get this junk off my face."

Half an hour later Scissors Kildane dropped the boys off at the hotel and thanked them again. In the lobby they met Pat Reynolds and a stranger. Chip didn't recognize Stu Gardner until the Drake scout slapped him on the back.

"Mr. Gardner! I'm sure glad to see you! I didn't know you were here!"

"Oh, yes, I've been around," Gardner said quietly.

"By the way, boys, we saw the program. You fellows were knockouts!"

"I ought to knock someone out," Biggie said, glaring at Soapy.

"Did you really like it?" Soapy asked innocently.

Gardner nodded. "We sure did! Particularly the part where Chip and Gordon, here, were talking about the game tomorrow night. By the way, Chip," Gardner warned, "Johnny's tough! He's got an awful lot of fast stuff. You'd better be right tomorrow night. In the meantime, I don't want to keep you fellows up late. We'll get together tomorrow or the next day, Chip. I've got a lot of things to tell you."

"Let's hit the hay," Biggie suggested. "We've got to be in shape tomorrow night or we're gonna be goin' home on the midnight express."

Chip, however, couldn't get to sleep. The brief taste of professional baseball, the television, the exciting life Kildane lived, and the atmosphere of good-fellowship had flooded him with dreams of his own future. College seemed far away at the moment. Then he thought of his mother, and her intense desire for him to get a college education, and he thought about Biggie and Soapy and his pals at home who had planned so long on going up to State together and, as Soapy would say, "taking over!" There was "the Rock" too. His old high school coach who was now moving up to the university as Frosh coach of football, basketball, and baseball.

Chip had never been to a football training camp, but he had received an invitation to Lake Sundown, State's fall camp, which was to start Monday, September 12th. Chip's four buddies had been invited, too. Biggie and Soapy and Speed Morris and Red Schwartz. Chip's thoughts shifted to football and the thrill of competing against other fellows for a place on the starting team. Gosh, there would be fifty fellows on hand . . . maybe a hundred. All freshmen and all trying out for the team. College was a lot different from high school. When a fellow went to college he was supposed to grow up, assume responsibilities, get ready for the future. . . .

CHAPTER 3

BIRD-DOG BONUS TRICK

PLAYER SCOUTING is undoubtedly the most expensive
item in big-league baseball. But it is vitally important
to the success of any chain, and the managers and the
owners of big-league teams are fully aware of the fact.
That explained the presence in Parkville of the fifty or
more baseball experts who were there expressly for the
purpose of viewing the amateur tournament sponsored
and promoted by Eddie Duer. Scouting for big-league
players is a serious business, and scouts have to deliver
or look for another job. Each big-league outfit spends
about a quarter of a million dollars a year to support
the scouting pay roll, plus the same amount for travel-
ing expenses, and another quarter of a million for player
bonuses. A good estimate of the expense to a big-league
team for scouting, promoting, and a training camp for
youngsters is half a million dollars. Every big-league
chain has twenty or thirty year-round men in its scouting department and ten or fifteen bird dogs or spare-
time scouts.

Scouts are a friendly and loquacious tribe. And when
they get together, a thousand stories of players discovered and signed are told and retold. In the early

24

days of organized baseball great discoveries were easy to sign. That is no longer true. Outstanding players are known to practically every scouting organization, now, and the discovery of a gold nugget is almost impossible. Today, the big job is to outbid the competing scouts and cultivate the favor of the boy. That means talking to the boy's family, his friends, the minister, and the kid's high school coach; selling all those persons in order to get the boy's signature on a contract.

After the youngsters had headed for bed, the scouts and fans remaining in the lobby began to talk about the visiting players and the Bears and Mules and the close race between the two teams. Stu Gardner was there talking to some of his friends. Gabby Breen tried to maneuver close to Pat Reynolds, but Stu Gardner blocked every move Breen made, to the great amusement of Reynolds. Pat knew all about Gabby Breen and he was determined to co-operate with Gardner in every way possible in order that Chip Hilton and Biggie Cohen might be protected from the tricky scout. Later that evening Reynolds surprised Gardner by asking him to sit in the Plainsmen dugout during the tournament.

"Isn't it against the rules?" Gardner asked.

"No, just as long as you don't talk business to one of the kids. And I guess we don't have to worry about that."

"You can say that again," Gardner agreed. "I'm only interested in Hilton and Cohen and I had an understanding with them long ago. But when those two kids finish college—"

Despite Chip's almost sleepless night, he was awake at the crack of dawn. He pulled Soapy and Biggie out of bed despite their protests and led the way to the cafeteria. After breakfast they headed for the stadium to watch the Laker–Cornhusker game. The Lakers were far too strong for the Cornhuskers and won easily, 12 to 7. After lunch the three boys were right back in the stands when the Hillbillies and the Miners tangled. This game was tense and tight, a pitchers' duel all the way, with the Miners winning 1 to 0.

The Yankee–Buckeye game was close and interesting, but in the top of the seventh, when the crowd stood up for the stretch, Chip and Biggie and Soapy and the rest of the Plainsmen started for the dressing room to get ready for their own game with the Rebels. After they were suited-up, Reynolds took time to run through the respective strength and the weaknesses of the Rebels and then let them watch the last inning of the Yankee–Buckeye game which the Northerners won, 6 to 3.

Dusk was falling when the Plainsmen took the field for their hitting practice and the lights flashed on, battery by battery, until, at seven-thirty, all the lights were ablaze and the stands were beginning to fill with spectators. Bear Stadium was a first-class ball park with a well-constructed grandstand and long rows of bleachers stretching from first and third bases nearly to the bull pens in the left- and right-hand corners. Chip walked out beside the mound and threw two or three balls to the hitters just to get the feel of the background. But Reynolds called him back.

"Get out of there! You're liable to get hit! You work out over here in front of the dugout."

While Chip was warming up, Reynolds sat beside Gardner in the dugout. "I think we can win the whole thing, Stu," Pat said confidently, "that is, if I can get two good games out of Hilton."

"You'll get two good games from Chip, all right, Pat," Gardner said grimly. "He's the best kid chucker I've ever seen. If he's right, you won't have any trouble with any of these teams. What are your plans?"

"I plan to work Chip tonight, of course, and then try that Parcels boy you were telling me about in the next one and then come back with Hilton on Saturday. That will give him three good days of rest and he ought to be okay."

"He'll be all right. By the way, you'd better get busy. It won't be long now."

A few minutes later the Rebels took the field and Chip put on his warm-up jacket and sat down in a corner of the dugout. Reynolds sat down beside him and put his arm across Chip's shoulders. "Chip," he said, "this is your big game. I know you've had some night-game experience and I heard Kildane give you those tips last night, and everything he said was right. Use your fast stuff early. Get the jump on them if you can and stay with the hard ones until they get used to the lights and then you can use your twisters and soft stuff. Beyond that, I want you to pitch your own game. Are you right?"

"I sure feel right, Coach. I'm good and loose and my arm feels swell."

"Good! We've got a good hitting team, Chip, and I don't think you'll have to bear down all the way, but you'd better stay ahead during the first inning or two. Another thing, you've got a good fielding team behind you, so don't try to do it all yourself. Right?"

"Right, Coach," Chip said firmly. Would it be all right for Soapy to work with me?"

"Of course, Chip. If you want Soapy, well, Soapy it is! I'll probably work him for five innings and end it up with Overton. Get together with the two of them and go over your signs. We don't want any slip-ups. Good luck, Chip. Give 'em all you've got."

Up in the stands, Gabby Breen was right back in the middle of his friends of the previous day and it seemed almost as though the conversation had never been interrupted.

"There's your big lefty out there on first," someone said.

Breen watched Biggie as the Plainsmen whipped the ball around the bases and, as he watched, his shrewd eyes narrowed. The concentration of the voluble scout did not pass unnoticed.

"Well?" someone asked.

Breen was cautious. "Not bad," he said good-humoredly, "but anyone can play catch."

Just at that instant Biggie took one of Skinny White's throws from deep short. The ball was far to Biggie's right and the big left-hander shifted his feet with lightning speed, extended himself in a full stretch, and made a successful glove-hand stab. Then, gathering his feet under himself skillfully, he pivoted rapidly and fired the ball straight as a string to Soapy Smith straddling third base. It was big-league stuff and Breen knew it. So did the fans surrounding the flashy stranger.

"Anyone can do that, too, eh?" the same voice persisted.

"No-o-o," Breen drawled, "not everybody. But let's have a look-see at his hittin'."

Then Breen shifted his eyes to the Plainsmen's bench and the keen eyes of the scout narrowed angrily as he studied Stu Gardner. "No ethics," he muttered to himself, "absolutely no ethics." A few moments later the game was on and Breen concentrated on the play and on the slender towheaded chucker who toed the rubber for the Plainsmen.

Seconds later Breen had forgotten Stu Gardner, the friendly fans who surrounded him, and everything else as he watched the kid in the box rear back, kick a long leg toward third base, uncoil, and throw a blur of light down the alley with effortless ease. Before Chip had thrown a dozen pitches to the plate, Breen was elbowing the man next to him.

"What's that kid's name? The pitcher out there?"

"Kid by the name of Hilton. Got a great reputation in his home state."

When the Plainsmen trotted in for their time at bat and the Rebels took the field, Breen was sitting on the extreme edge of the wooden seat, eyes glued on the tall, graceful youngster with the wide, sloping, power-packed shoulders who was making his way toward the Plainsmen's dugout.

"Three up and three down," Breen muttered, "and they ain't seen it yet!"

Gabby Breen hardly looked at the Plainsmen's hitters, didn't even know it when they managed to push a run around so Chip would have something to work on. Breen watched Chip and Gardner as a cat watches a mouse and he was puzzled. When Gardner neither looked at nor spoke to the kid pitcher, he was even more puzzled.

"What's the score?" he muttered. "That Gardner's no dumbbell. How come he's in the dugout? That fox ain't sittin' down there in that hole just to keep outta the dew."

Breen continued to worry as Chip kept mowing down the Rebel hitters. As the innings passed, with Chip steadily fashioning a no-hitter, Breen's pasty complexion took on a pink hue and his heart kept thumping faster and faster against his ribs. Gabby had known lots of young chuckers who could go for five, or six, or even seven innings, but this kid got stronger all the time. And when a third strike got away from Soapy Smith and the hitter went all the way to third on Soapy's bad throw to second, Breen noted that the kid on the mound lost none of his poise.

Suddenly it was the bottom of the ninth and the big kid was fogging the ball past the hitters as if he were in a hurry to get home. With the last pitch, Gabby Breen was on his feet, cheering the youngster and watching the Plainsmen who were pulling and pommeling Chip Hilton and yelling excitedly with the sheer joy that the true baseball fan expresses when a hurler chalks up a no-hitter.

Breen glanced at the row of goose eggs in the Rebel frames, stretching clear across the scoreboard, but he never noticed the five runs and the nine hits the Plainsmen had collected. For the first time in many a ball game, Gabby Breen didn't know the score. As he hurried toward the exit, his thoughts were concerned with an important telephone call he had to make and it never occurred to him that he had completely forgotten Biggie Cohen, the star first sacker.

Breen had difficulty locating his party, but finally, long past midnight, he was rewarded, and he hustled into the telephone booth in the lobby. Gabby was a careful person with respect to his varied enterprises, and he left nothing to chance. That was the reason for the telephone-booth call instead of the comfort of a call from his own room.

As he waited, Breen drummed his fingers on the metal coin box. This had been a good day. He knew now that there were two possible big-league sensations here in Parkville and he meant to tie them up. He had concentrated on Biggie Cohen first, simply because he had a deal lined up to produce a good first sacker. But he had almost jumped out of his flashy shirt when he had noticed Chip's delivery and had seen the big, broad-shouldered kid pouring his fast one down the alley. The boy's effortless fast ball reminded him of Bob Feller in the "speed-merchant's" first years in the big leagues. His thoughts were disrupted by the completion of his call to Boots Rines, and before he realized it he was shouting.

"Look, Boots, the kid's got it! Throws a fireball. Throws it easy, too! No lungin'. He's more'n fast! You know he's throwin' a baseball, 'cause you can see it when the other kids chuck it around, but when he drops that long arm of his back of his leg and spins and kicks his left toe—brother, you don't see no more baseball! Throws a marble down that alley! Why, the kid catcher he's workin' with can't even hold him. . . .

"I seen him in there first time tonight and I gotta move fast. That guy Gardner's up here and he don't hang 'round a jerkwater town like this just because he likes to chase butterflies. . . . No siree, Boots, I gotta have the cash! . . . Yeah! . . . Send me a cashier's check. I can get it cashed here! . . .

"When? . . . Can't you make it sooner? . . . All right! But hurry! This deal calls for the old suitcase trick and it's gotta be big and fast! Only break we got is Gardner. He's stupid, too straight-laced for his own good. That's why I know he—

"That's what I'm tryin' to tell you. Gardner wouldn't break his word if it cost him his life and that's why I know he hasn't signed the kid up. He'll probably beat it for the kid's home town right after the game Saturday afternoon. . . .

"Valley Falls. I know where it is, but I'm gonna leech the kid and sell him before he gets home. . . . Look, I can twist him around my finger. Leave it to me. He

won't get out of my sight. You rush that dough, okay?
. . . S'long!"

Early-morning rising was old stuff to Chip Hilton.
His Sugar Bowl job in Valley Falls had required that
he open the sweetshop before he went to school and it
was a matter of habit for him to rise early. So, it wasn't
strange that he should wake early the following morning and promptly pull the covers off his companions and
laugh at their sleepy, yawn-punctuated protests.

"Gettin' up in the middle of the night," Soapy
grumbled. "Where you goin', anyway? What's the rush?
We don't play till this afternoon!"

"Yeah, and Reynolds said to sleep late," Biggie added.
"Of course you don't have to work today, so you can
take it easy."

"What's the program for this mornin', anyway?"
Soapy demanded.

"Skull practice in Room 2B at ten," Chip explained,
"lunch at eleven, and on the field at one o'clock. Come
on. We've got to get some breakfast and get a little
exercise."

"Exercise!" Soapy yelled. "Who wants exercise? Not
me, brother!"

But Chip persisted, and after breakfast and the
"walk," they were just in time to make Pat Reynolds'
skull practice at ten o'clock. Reynolds was late, but it
didn't matter to the Plainsmen. They were reading the
story of the game in the morning papers. But they
weren't too busy to greet their three teammates from
Valley Falls.

"Hiya, Chip! You see the papers?"

"Look! They got your picture plastered all over the
page!"

"Nice hitting, Biggie. Here! Read the story!"

"What's the paper say about me?" Soapy demanded. "What's the matter with those pen pushers? Don't they give catchers no credit?"

Pat Reynolds arrived at that moment and checked Soapy's tirade. The next hour was devoted to a study of the notes Reynolds and Stu Gardner had prepared on the Yankee hitters and the team's fielding weaknesses.

Like Chip, Gabby Breen didn't sleep late that morning, either. He had lots to do and he wasn't going to waste any time. He spent most of the morning in the morgue of the Parkville *Gazette* checking the sports pages of the Valley Falls *Times* and *Post*. Gabby Breen wanted to know more about one William "Chip" Hilton. He was amazed by what he discovered. He couldn't understand why big-league scouts hadn't been lurking on the Hilton porch for the past three years. How could a kid like that be overlooked? Breen couldn't help thinking about the story which concerned a Detroit scout who had reputedly signed Hal Newhouser for five hundred dollars and had no sooner wrapped up the contract when two Cleveland scouts appeared with a bonus check for fifteen thousand dollars made out to the order of Newhouser.

The thought disturbed Breen and he passed a restless morning, scanning paper after paper and reading about Chip Hilton. When the Plainsmen took the field that afternoon, Breen was in his usual seat, watching Chip loosen up and observing every move Cohen made on first base. The longer Gabby thought about the two kids the more impatient he became. He wished Rines would hurry up with that money. Maybe he should have called Kearns direct. If he didn't get the dough tonight, he *would* call Kearns.

"Sign anyone up?" one of the fans asked curiously.

"No, not yet," Breen admitted slowly, "but I've got my mind made up on two, three—" He eyed his questioner. "You know, we got sort of a gentleman's agreement not to try to sign any of these kids until they get back to their homes."

"The big first baseman one of them?" a fan persisted.

"Yes and no," Breen fenced, "but I can tell you one thing. I can spot a good prospect quick as anyone. Some guys gotta follow a kid around all year. Not me!"

"How about the kid who pitched the no-hitter yesterday? Bet you got your eye on him," someone said chidingly.

Breen smiled mysteriously. "Could be," he said. "He could be one of them and then it could be someone else."

"Well," someone said cynically, "you'll have a tough time signing some of the babies they got in this tournament. There's a lot of big operators hanging around, you've got lots of competition."

Breen laughed loudly. "Yeah? Let me tell you something, my friend. I can get any player I want! Look, I been in this game a long time. Here's the way I work on 'em."

Breen leaned closer to the surrounding heads and lowered his voice. "When I'm after a guy, see, I know what it takes before I make a move. Sometimes I work it one way and sometimes I work it another. One of my special tricks is what I call the suitcase gag. I make a date with a kid in his own home, see, usually at night so his folks will be around. Then I turn up carryin' a suitcase, see? And after I've talked to them, see? And got them interested, got 'em all ears— Right then, I leans down suddenlike, and I opens the suitcase and I dumps ten thousand dollars—or whatever amount it is—right out on the floor! Right on the floor! That gets 'em! Right then I says: 'Sign this contract!' Then I shove the contract under their noses and before you can say Jackie Robinson I got the kid sealed, signed, and delivered. Smart, eh?"

Breen's listeners nodded. They liked this inside stuff. And they gazed at Breen with new respect in their eyes.

Breen leaned back, satisfied with his performance. He noted the awe in the faces of his listeners and he almost chuckled aloud. These birds didn't know it, but he'd been putting on a little rehearsal for a kid by the name of Chip Hilton.

CHAPTER 4

STAR BULL-PEN ROOKIE

SOAPY SMITH was standing in the center of the players' tunnel leading to the field. Soapy was anxious to get out on the field. He spat in his glove and thumped the pocket with the closed fist of his right hand. Soapy had been muttering to himself. Now he gestured toward center field. "Well," he opined smugly, "now we know who we have to beat for the big cup, come Saturday afternoon!"

"Cut it," Biggie growled. "You wanta jinx us?"

Chip glanced at the scoreboard. It was the last of the ninth, no one on, two down, two strikes on the batter, and the Miners were leading the Lakers, 4 to 3. And that's the way the game ended, the Miners thus becoming one of the tournament finalists. Minutes later the Yankees were hitting. Then the Plainsmen took their licks and fielding practice and came running when Reynolds called for a huddle in front of the dugout.

"All right, kids," Reynolds began briskly. "This is it! Parcels! You start! Overton! You work behind the plate! Here's the batting order: White, Degnan, Maneri, Cohen, Chambers, Erickson, Roberts, Overton, and Parcels. Now—let's go!"

Reynolds ordered Soapy, Chip, Sheffer, and Lennox out to the bull pen with instructions for Soapy to have Sheffer and Lennox ready.

"Chip, you throw just enough to loosen up. You won't be doing any pitching today but I may use you as a pinch hitter."

Chip had never been in a regular bull pen in his life. It was a strange feeling to watch his teammates from the left-field corner. A fellow seemed too far away to be of much help, and Chip wanted especially to cheer Kip Parcels. He would always remember the little right-hander's sportsmanship in the championship game just two months ago when Valley Falls and Salem had fought a nineteen-inning battle for the championship of the state. Salem had won that game and Chip had lost the pitchers' duel to Kip when a batted ball lit foul, spun into fair territory, and enabled a runner on third to score the winning run. But the memory of Kip Parcels' gracious sportsmanship had eased a lot of the sting of defeat.

After a few throws Chip sat down on the bench facing the infield to watch the game. A few minutes later Soapy, Bill Sheffer, and Bob Lennox joined him and the three boys sat watching Kip Parcels' masterful pitching. The little chucker was great, never in trouble. When the Plainsmen came in for their turn at bat in the bottom of the sixth, leading by a 5–0 score, Reynolds sent Rick Williams out to tell Soapy to get Bob Lennox ready to pitch and to come in with him to catch the rest of the game.

"Oh, boy!" Soapy barked. "C'mon, Bob! Let's go!"

Then, with every pitch, Soapy began to chant his newest rhyme: "Chip, Kip, Bob, or Bill— If one doesn't do it, the other will!"

Soapy was still chanting when he and Bob Lennox

started for the diamond and Ken Overton trudged out to the bull pen.

"Nice going, Ken," Chip said. "Kip must have been great."

"He *was* that!" Overton agreed. "Coach sent him to the showers."

The Yankees sent Bob Lennox to the showers, too, in the top of the ninth. They began one of those unexplainable hitting sprees, scoring two runs and filling the bases with none down before Reynolds called "time" and waved for Bill Sheffer.

"Gee, that's tough on Bob," Overton said sympathetically. "This team is death on southpaws, and they like soft stuff. Kip and I found that out right off the bat."

"Bill's fast," Chip said calmly. "He'll take care of them."

Sheffer took care of them, just as Chip said he would. Pitching like a big-league bull-pen fireman, he struck out the first man he faced, and forced the next hitter to send a weak ground ball to Dutch Degnan, who fielded it cleanly and made the sure play at first for the second out. The runner on third scampered home, making it: Plainsmen 5, Yankees 3.

That left two on, runners on second and third, and two away. But Sheffer was the master. He kept ahead of the Yankee hitter and won the game himself by fielding a high hopper and making the throw to Biggie Cohen for the third out and the game.

Biggie stomped the sack with his size-fourteen spikes and headed for the dugout to give Bill Sheffer a southpaw slap on the back with his hamlike hand and to shove the ball into his glove.

"Try that on your piano, Bill," Biggie said happily. "Boy, you earned it."

Chip and Ken Overton got there just in time to join the gang in giving Sheffer a cheer and then the Plainsmen rushed for the dressing room. Soapy voiced their thoughts. "Now for the Miners and the championship!"

That would have been enough baseball in one day for most people. It was for most of the Plainsmen. But it wasn't enough for Chip Hilton, Biggie Cohen, and Soapy Smith. They had caught the fervent baseball fever which gripped Parkville's citizens, and right after a steak dinner they started for Bear Stadium. Pat Reynolds had lifted his curfew for the night because this was Thursday and the championship game wasn't scheduled until Saturday afternoon.

The Midwestern League is composed of eight clubs, each one owned by a big-league chain. For that reason, the teams are manned by a few old-timers, players past their peak, but chiefly by hustling youngsters, rookies, and other hopefuls who are being tested and primed for big-league action. This year, the race had been a dogfight all the way between the Parkville Bears and the Hedgetown Mules. The game tonight, therefore, was an important one and both managers were using their best chucker. "Eagle Beak" Eddie Duer had named Scissors Kildane as the Bears' starting pitcher, and Boots Rines had elected to go with Lefty Turner, the pride of the Mules.

Chip could hardly wait for the tall chucker to start the game. He studied the Bear line-up displayed on the scoreboard in center field and listened to the enthusiastic Parkville rooters as they talked about their favorite players.

"Eddie's startin' his strongest club. Wants to win this one bad."

"Eddie wants to win 'em all!"

"Just look at that line-up and tell me what's holdin' 'em up. The only player with any real experience is Curry."

"You know why Mickey Curry's here, don't you?"

"Sure, because the Drakes want an experienced catcher handling Eddie's kid chuckers."

"Well, wouldn't you want an old hand behind the plate to develop sure-fire big-leaguers like Kildane and Akers?"

"What's wrong with Softy Richards and Windy?"

"Aw, Softy's too small. Besides, he doesn't throw that hard one."

"Windy throws a hard one!"

"Sure, but where? He's just as liable to throw it over the grandstand as over the plate."

"All lefties are like that if they're fast!"

"Phil Akers isn't a lefty and he's sure wild enough."

"He's not wild! Heck, his wildness helps him more than it hurts him. Hitters don't take no toe holds when he's chuckin'."

"Me, I like Kildane!"

"Who doesn't?"

Chip studied the batting order of the Bears and compared the list with his program. Corky Squill, the lead-off hitter, was listed as five-nine and weighing one hundred and eighty pounds. Bucky Boyd, the "push-along" shortstop, was listed precisely the same. Chip glanced at the infield. The double-play combination looked exactly like twins from where he sat. Bill Dawson, batting third and playing left field, was listed at an even six feet and one hundred and ninety pounds. The cleanup hitter was Stretch Johnson. It was easy to see where Johnson got his nickname. The tall first sacker seemed to be all arms but didn't look as though he weighed one hundred and eighty-five pounds. Chip's guess was that Johnson was about as tall as Biggie. Chip shifted his eyes to the outfield again. Norm Klein in center field and Ted Smith in right were each listed at six-one and a hundred and ninety-five. They moved fast and had good arms.

Third base was patrolled by a short, active player who gunned the ball across to Stretch Johnson on a string. Chip studied Paul Hale intently. He'd heard a lot about Hale. The five-ten youngster weighed only a hundred and fifty pounds, but he was already tabbed as another Red Rolfe. Then Chip focused on the catcher, Mickey Curry. The burly receiver batted in the eighth spot and was the captain of the team. He was listed as six-two, two hundred and ten pounds, and he had an arm that was *an arm*.

Soapy followed Chip's glance and then elbowed Biggie. "Ever see anyone throw like that?" he demanded.

Biggie shook his head. "Nope," he said admiringly, "I never saw anyone throw like that, and I don't see how they can keep him out of the big time."

"Bats .380, says here," Soapy added.

Right then, the Bears came dashing off the field and the band in the grandstand began its concert.

A minute later the plate umpire held up his hands and announced the batteries, and the Bears trotted out to their positions. Kildane was last out of the dugout and every Parkville rooter leaped to his feet and joined his voice in the tribute to the Bears' great hurler.

"Yea, Kildane! Yea, Scissors!"

"Oh, you, Scissors!"

"Come on, you Bears!"

Kildane was fast, as fast as lightning. His long throwing arm reached nearly to the ground when he pointed his left toe toward third base, and when he pivoted around and took his stride, he seemed to reach right across the plate.

Butch Bates led off for the Mules, crowding the plate, looking for a walk. But he didn't have a chance. Kildane's fast ball darted down across the plate three straight times and the chunky shortstop was called out on strikes. Sandy Adams and Nick Marreno followed suit. Three up and three down and the crowd cheered Kildane every step of the way to the dugout. Chip and Soapy and Biggie cheered right to the last, too.

Corky Squill, the Bears' chunky second sacker, led off for the home team and on the first pitch electrified everyone in the stadium by banging a three-bagger to right center. Lefty Turner, the Mules' Number One chucker, didn't like that and added to his woes by walking Bucky Boyd. That brought Bill Dawson up and the lefty left fielder brought the home crowd to its feet again by doubling off the right-field wall and the Bears had two runs. Turner settled down then, struck out Johnson and Klein, and forced Ted Smith to fly out to Bernie Roth in left field.

Scissors Kildane's mastery over the Mules held. The big fellow seemed tireless and, as inning after inning passed, he continued to control the game. Lefty Turner never recovered from his bad start. Two hours and twenty minutes later, the Bears had won by a score of 6 to 1 and had increased their lead in the win column by three games with two less defeats in the important loss column.

Chip was glad the Bears had won, for several reasons. First, because of his admiration for Scissors Kildane. Second, because the Mules turned out to be a hard-losing outfit. Then, too, Lefty Turner had used a vicious duster, forcing the Bear hitters to back away from the plate all through the game. Chip could understand a chucker moving back a batter who crowded the plate, got out of the batter's box, but to aim the ball deliberately at opposing players' heads, for no reason other than the inability to check their hitting, was poor sportsmanship. Turner was a sullen and vicious chucker and Chip was glad he had lost.

Chip grinned, though, when he thought of Corky Squill. Turner had dusted Corky off and the stocky second baseman had charged out to the mound waving his bat and had chased the Mules' pitching star clear back to second base. The incident had struck Chip as being peculiar, because, in the field, Squill hadn't opened his mouth nor made an unnecessary move.

Most keystone guardians are "holler" players, who spark-plug the whole team. But not Corky Squill. He was a chunk of ice. He never batted an eyelash nor made a move after he assumed his position. Bucky Boyd was just the opposite. The hustling, bustling shortstop was never quiet, thumping his glove, moving his feet, and starting one way or another on every pitch.

Later that night, when the lights were out and Chip was trying to go to sleep, he was still thinking about the game and about the Bears. Maybe someday he'd be a pitcher like Scissors Kildane . . . after college maybe. . . .

The next afternoon Chip and Soapy and Biggie were back in the same seats in the stadium and again they were pulling and rooting for the Bears. But the Mules were fighting tooth and nail now, realizing that every game with the Bears was doubly important, and using every trick in the deck. Once again, it was Corky Squill and Scissors Kildane who starred.

Squill had another perfect day at bat, scoring two of the Bears' three runs himself, and driving in the third. In the field he was brilliant, making four spectacular

stops and teaming up with Bucky Boyd and Stretch
Johnson to complete three sensational twin-killings.
Chip marveled at Squill's immobility in his position.
The bowlegged infielder seemed almost asleep, once he
set himself, but when a play developed he was chain
lightning.

In the top of the ninth, with the Bears leading 3 to 2
and two away, Softy Richards got into trouble. He hit
Sandy Adams, walked Nick Marreno, and pitched himself into a two-and-nothing hole with Jack Fellows, the
Mules' cleanup hitter. Eddie Duer called "time" then,
and after a brief consultation with Richards, surprised
everyone in the ball park, except Scissors Kildane, when
he called the big fellow in from the bull pen. The
crowd went wild.

"Kildane! He's gonna use Kildane!"

"Don't get it! Scissors worked yesterday!"

"Duer's nuts! He'll *ruin* the kid!"

"Shut up! Eddie knows what he's doin'!"

Eddie Duer knew what he was doing, all right. So
did Scissors Kildane. The tall chucker didn't fool
around. He breezed five fast warm-up pitches across the
plate, waited until Fellows stepped up there, and then
broke a twister across the outside corner for a called
strike. Completely ignoring the base runners, Scissors
burned a fast one across Fellows' wrists which the Mule
slugger went for too late. Every person in the stadium
was on his feet now, tense and tight and breathless, as
Kildane toed the rubber and took his stretch. But Scissors took care of that, dropped his hands to his belt, and
held them there for a long second. Then he twisted his
body, kicked his long leg, pivoted with lightning speed,
and threw his knuckler.

Jack Fellows, trying to outguess Kildane, had figured
a fast one, and had started his swing. When he saw the

knuckler, he checked his bat and made a desperate effort to knock the floating ball out of the park. But all his bat hit was the breeze, and Mickey Curry had the ball in his hip pocket and was on his way to the dugout before Fellows realized that he had nearly broken his back for nothing, that he had missed the ball by a full mile, struck out with two aboard, and lost his chance to win the game.

The emotion-charged fans were on their way before the ball ended up in Curry's glove. They surged over the barriers, out on the field, heading for Kildane. Their hero had won another game and they wanted to show their appreciation by touching him, lifting him on their shoulders, cheering him to the skies.

The celebration didn't end on the field. That night, wherever anyone went, he heard Parkville's citizens talking about their team and about Scissors Kildane and Eddie Duer and Corky Squill and Mickey Curry and Softy Richards.

Chip and his buddies got to bed early, determined to be in tiptop shape for the championship game the next afternoon. But down below, in the lobby, the coffee shop, and the grill, the scouts gathered and compared notes. Only Gabby Breen was missing.

Success in player scouting is no longer a matter of hustle and acumen; it has become a battle of personalities and bankrolls in the auction ring. And the high dollar bonus for signing the contract is the come-on, the clincher which lands the potential big-league star.

Gabby Breen used the mighty dollar, too. But in a different way. Gabby liked to be secretive and dramatic and he was eager to try his trickery on Chip Hilton. Furthermore, he believed the end justified the means and was determined to disregard Eddie Duer's ruling with respect to approaching the players. But Breen couldn't move without ready cash, and he was nearly frantic because Boots Rines hadn't yet contacted the owner of the Mules, Hoot Kearns. That was the reason Breen had been on Rines' heels ever since the end of the game and the reason why he was now badgering Rines in the latter's room in the Park Hotel.

"Aw, Boots, what's the matter with you? You said I'd have the dough today! I gotta move fast! This kid's gonna be pullin' out of here tomorrow and you'll miss the boat on him just like you missed out on Scissors Kildane."

"Listen, Gabby," Rines explained patiently, "I told you I wrote Kearns and gave him the whole story. What more can I do? Don't forget I'm managin' a ball club, trying to win a pennant! I've got to concentrate on winning games!"

Breen's face was purple with anger and he could scarcely contain himself. "But this kid's the real article! You're actin' just like you did last year. Bullheaded! And that's why you're in second place and gettin' nowhere fast. If you'd listened to me last year you woulda had Scissors Kildane and you woulda had the pennant clinched weeks ago. You're gonna keep on foolin' around and end up out of a job!"

"That's enough, Gabby!" Rines snapped. "I've contacted Kearns and the rest is up to him. Good night!"

Breen stalked out of the room and headed straight for the nearest telephone. Boots Rines probably didn't suspect it, but he had incurred the bitter enmity of an unscrupulous man, a man who was determined to do everything in his power to undermine Rines with the owner of the Mules, hoping to win the job for himself. Yes, Gabby Breen wanted Rines' job as manager of the Mules and he meant to get it. Boots had had his chance. Gabby was looking out for Number One!

CHAPTER 5

MOST VALUABLE PLAYER

H. B. KEARNS, owner of the Hedgetown Mules, was one of those patrons of baseball who believed in a hands-off policy where the manager of his team was concerned. In many instances, however, personal policies must be governed by financial considerations. Unfortunately that was the case with respect to Kearns' ownership of the Mules. Hedgetown fans loved a winner, but they wouldn't support a loser, and Hoot Kearns couldn't afford the doubtful luxury of a losing ball club. Last year's success had gone to the heads of Hedgetown's fans and they couldn't understand why the Mules, the champions, should play second fiddle to the Bears. Particularly since the players representing the Bears were mostly youngsters, first-year rookies. Boots Rines, the manager of the Mules, had made no additions to his player roster and Hedgetown's fans had looked forward to a runaway race. But when the Bears took the lead and held it right down the stretch, the fans became disgusted and began looking for a "goat."

Gabby Breen had been quick to realize the possibilities in the attitude of the Mule rooters and had proceeded to fan the flames. He repeatedly and diplomatically referred to Boots Rines' "tough luck" in failing to take advantage of the opportunity to sign Scissors Kildane and Corky Squill, and he always followed that up by stating that Rines was too good to his players and didn't bear down enough.

"You know," Breen would say hesitantly, "maybe I shouldn't be talkin' this way—and I sure wish Boots nothing but the best—but it might be the best thing that ever happened to Rines if Kearns should give him a rest. Now this is strictly confidential and I know you won't repeat it—Rines is losing his grip. He's on the verge of a nervous breakdown."

The Hedgetown fans had fallen hard for that kind of "confidential" information, and the failure of the Mules to gain ground on the fast-moving Bears had further added to their increasing demands for a change. And since the only possible change which could be made was the ousting of the team's manager, Boots Rines inevitably became the goat the fans had been seeking.

Hoot Kearns had tried to appease the fans and the crusading writers who were demanding a new pilot, but his support of Rines merely added to the fire of the opposition. The pressure of the public and baseball writers, together with the recent double loss to the Bears, had just about forced a showdown. That was the reason Kearns had shown up at his office at such an early hour on Saturday morning. That could have been the reason why Gabby Breen's telephone call fired his temper.

"Hilton?" Kearns repeated testily. "Never heard of him! . . . What letter? . . . You mean better than Kildane? . . . How much will you need? . . . Seems like a lot of money. . . . All right, all right, I'll get it off right away. I can't understand why I haven't heard from Boots, though. What happened yesterday? . . .

Well, there's only sixteen games left, counting today, and eight of the sixteen are against the Bears. What happens when we play that team? . . .

"Oh, I know all about Kildane. Seems like all I've heard all year's been Kildane and Squill. . . . Never mind all that. You'd better arrange to get back here next Thursday or Friday. I might have to do something about Eddie before we play here on the twentieth. Every baseball fan in town's been on my neck. You think you could take charge starting with our game here with the Bears? . . .

"There isn't anyone else and you know it. . . . That's better! Naturally, I want Boots to finish out the season. But if he keeps losing I'll have to do something about it. . . . All right, you be ready! But don't you breathe a word of this to anyone. Understand? I might not have to let him go. . . . Good. I'll be expecting you Thursday or Friday at the latest. Right? . . . Good-bye, then."

Gabby Breen hung up the receiver and stood motionless in the telephone booth. He scarcely dared breathe for fear he'd wake up and find it was all a dream. Kearns was all but offering him Rines' job. Why, by this time next week he might be bossing the Mules . . . would for sure if they kept losing. . . .

While Gabby Breen had been making his call, Chip was talking to his mother in Valley Falls. Mary Hilton had phoned to wish him luck in the game and to find out if he was all right. Most youngsters feign annoyance when their parents worry about them, but way down deep they like it. Chip Hilton's whole life was wrapped up in his mother and her happiness, and he wouldn't have dreamed of enjoying a pleasure or a success without sharing it with her.

Chip was thinking about his mother all through Pat

Reynolds' skull practice that morning, and she was in his thoughts when he was introduced over the loud-speaker and stepped out in front of the dugout that afternoon beside his Plainsmen teammates. Then the band played "The Star-Spangled Banner," and Chip took off his cap and held it in front of the letters on his baseball shirt and looked steadily at the flag waving so proudly above the scoreboard in center field. Before he realized it, he had finished his warm-up pitches and was standing back of the mound, looking down the alley at Soapy. Biggie's booming "Pour it on 'em, Chip-per" made him feel strong and ready, and he pulled his cap a little lower over his left eye and toed the rubber.

Chip Hilton had been just another kid pitcher to Parkville baseball fans a few days ago, before his open-ing game no-hitter. That performance had endeared him to these baseball enthusiasts and the thunderous cheer which greeted him came from the heart. About the only persons in that sellout crowd who didn't cheer the lithe young pitcher were the scouts in the stands who were mentally kicking themselves and their faulty scouting files which had failed to list William Hilton of Valley Falls. Gabby Breen watched his contemporaries closely, and when he saw their intent interest in the kid chucker, he began to abuse Boots Rines under his breath, and his angry thoughts provided his willing conscience with full justification for his machinations in securing Rines' job. Breen's thoughts were inter-rupted by the crowd-talk of the surrounding fans.

"Best kid pitcher *I* ever saw!"

"You can say that again! He's ready for this league right now!"

"Wonder how come a kid like that hasn't been signed up?"

"Beats me!"

Gabby Breen was perspiring freely now, and his pasty complexion had turned pink. His glance shot toward the Plainsmen dugout and his eyes narrowed as they focused on Stu Gardner. A tremendous cheer drew his eyes back to the field and he nudged the fan on his right. "What happened?" he asked.

"What's the matter with you? You blind? That's the kid's second straight strike-out. Two up and two down, just like that!"

The third hitter grounded weakly to Skinny White. The little shortstop scooped up the ball, and his underhand throw beat the runner by twenty feet. The crowd gave Chip another hand, and he lifted his cap awkwardly as he ducked into the friendly refuge of the dugout.

Just the same the Miners weren't knuckling down to the Plainsmen. Even though they couldn't get to Chip Hilton, they fought every inch of the way, and won the plaudits of the crowd by their brilliant defensive play. But the Plainsmen had too much power, and little by little the Miners began to crack. Chip felt stronger every inning, and going into the top of the eighth, with the Plainsmen leading 3 to 0, he had another no-hitter on the fire. Then, as so often happens, Chip's teammates began to pull for the perfect game, and unconsciously tightened up in their play. Chip realized suddenly, for the first time, that not a Miner had reached first base, and he, too, began to feel the strain. With two down, he got behind the hitter with a three-and-nothing count. Pat Reynolds wisely took a hand at that point. He had detected the familiar symptoms. He called "time," and substituted Ken Overton for Soapy Smith.

Chip realized that Reynolds was sparring for time, trying to give him a chance to settle down. The crowd knew it, too. The fans were tense, pulling for the tall towhead to make the grade. The plate umpire allowed Chip five pitches to Overton and then called "Play ball!" There was a heavy hush over the stadium as Chip took a full wind-up and threw his fast ball right across the middle of the plate for a called strike. Chip could almost feel the crowd's tension lift for a brief moment. Then it came right back.

Chip toed the rubber and sent another fast ball toward Overton's glove-target. But the ball never reached Overton. The batter caught that one just right, full on the nose. Chip saw the blur of the ball as it shot out and up like a streak of lightning over third base and headed for left field. He turned, slow motion, to watch the flight of the ball. Then he focused on the twinkling legs of Butch Maneri. Maneri wasn't even looking at the ball, he was heading at full speed for the extreme left corner of the field where the limed foul line met the fence. Just as he reached the fence Maneri leaped high in the air, made a backhand stab at the ball, and crashed into the fence. The crash was heard all over the field. But Maneri held the ball. Even as he fell, he held the glove-encased ball aloft.

The third-base umpire had followed the ball, was on top of the play, and jerked his thumb high for the out. The raising of the umpire's thumb seemed to release the crowd from mass hypnosis, for the roar which followed almost lifted the stands off their foundations. Butch Maneri's catch was the third out, but the plucky left fielder was out, too. The umpire called "time" until Butch came around, and Chip and Biggie, each with one of Maneri's arms draped over a shoulder, led him to the dugout. Then the cheering became one continuous roar.

The Plainsmen scored another run in the bottom of

the eighth to make the score 4 to 0. But the run wasn't needed. And the Plainsmen didn't need their last time at bat. Chip set the Miners down one, two, three to win the championship and receive credit for a perfect game —no hits, no walks, and sixteen strike-outs!

The Parkville fans gave Chip the Kildane treatment then, swarming out on the field and lifting him up on top of the dugout. They cheered and yelled until they had all of the Plainsmen up there and, next to Chip, Butch Maneri got the biggest hand. It took the Plainsmen half an hour to get to their dressing room, but they weren't kicking; they were the champs, and they liked it. Besides, they had no place to go except to the banquet, and Soapy Smith expressed their sentiments when he said, "We didn't come here to eat!"

Soapy's statement was a gross understatement. The banquet waiters would have testified to that with groans. In fact, it was nine-thirty before the speech-making began, and ten-thirty before the party reached its climax.

"I'm sure the boys will always appreciate the gold baseballs and the watches. But I'm sure they will treasure even more the wonderful hospitality the Parkville baseball fans have accorded them. As the coach of the Plainsmen I have been greatly privileged to work with such a fine group of young men and I shall always treasure this experience as the most enjoyable in my life."

Pat Reynolds received a tremendous ovation when he sat down and then William Malloy, the owner of the Bears, was introduced.

"This night culminates one of the most enjoyable weeks of my life. I think the only possible rival to this occasion will be the night we win this year's pennant—"

Malloy was drowned out, then, by a cheer and a

banging of fists on tables which threatened to break every piece of china in the room. When the enthusiasm finally subsided, Malloy continued.

"Now, it's my privilege to announce the name of the most valuable player—"

"Hilton! Chip Hilton!" Cries came from all over the banquet hall.

"Yea, Hilton! Yea, Chip Hilton!"

It took longer for the speaker to gain quiet this time. Chip's face was scarlet and his hands toyed nervously with his program.

"—no doubt about the choice nor the worthiness of the honor. William Hilton, it is my pleasure to present you with this plaque certifying your unanimous selection by the coaches, sportswriters, and the citizen's committee as the most valuable player in the tournament.

"Furthermore, a special award is offered to you by the management of the Parkville Bears which covers all your expenses as a special bench guest of the Bears for the balance of the season."

"Speech! We want Hilton! Speech!"

Chip got to his feet, somehow, and waited until the applause died away. He felt a tightness in his chest, and the words he spoke were in the voice of a stranger, hollow and faraway.

"Thank you, Mr. Malloy. I deeply appreciate the honor. I also want to express my thanks to Mr. Reynolds and to my teammates. It was swell to win the championship and it was swell to be on the same team with so many players who were so much more deserving of the honor as the most valuable player than I am."

Chip sat down then, almost overwhelmed by his feelings toward his teammates. He just couldn't understand why he couldn't put his thoughts into words.

But he needn't have worried. Every person in that

room knew what Chip had been trying to say and they appreciated his sportsmanship.

Later on, when the crowd was breaking up, Soapy and Biggie began to put pressure on Chip to take advantage of the opportunity to finish out the season with the Bears. These two friends were proud of their teammate. They knew how hard he had worked all through high school and how much the trip would mean to him. But Chip was thinking about someone else, about his mother, Mary Hilton. Chip had never been away from home and he wanted to be with his mother as much as possible before he started the four years at State.

"You could come home the last week, Chip," Biggie said. "The football camp doesn't open until September twelfth. You could stay with the team until the week before and still have a week at home."

"Sure, that's right," Soapy pointed out, "the league season ends on September fourth."

Chip was wavering, but it was Scissors Kildane who clinched the matter. He joined the three friends and went right to work on Chip.

"You're coming with us, aren't you?" he demanded. Then he answered his own question. "Of course you are! You'll learn a lot of baseball and I'll give you a lot of help with your chucking. Not that I know any more than your coach, but I can teach you some of the things I had to learn the hard way. Besides, you'll be in on the scene of the hottest baseball race in the country. The Mules beat the Leopards today, 8 to 1. Looks like it will be a dogfight right down to the wire. You'd better stick around. What do you say?"

"I'll ask my mother," Chip said hesitantly.

"Good!" Kildane said enthusiastically. "Come on! We'll call her right now! Let me talk to her! I'll sell her on the idea."

Mary Hilton didn't need Scissors Kildane to sell her on any idea which meant happiness to her son. "Of course he can stay," she said softly. "Of course. Let me talk to him."

While Chip was talking to his mother, Soapy, Biggie, and Kildane joined hands and danced around the room.

Chip tried to talk above the clamor. "They're crazy, Mother," he said. "Absolutely crazy! But I like it!"

The next afternoon Chip and his teammates sat in a special box behind the Parkville dugout and watched the Bears beat the Panthers 2 to 1 in a tight pitchers' duel. But when the game was over and his teammates and friends were gone, Chip waited alone, just a bit lonesome, until Kildane came hustling up, fresh from his shower, and hurried him out to the yellow convertible in the parking lot.

"Come on, kid," Kildane said happily, "we'll call your mother and have dinner with the gang and then see a show. You're going to see how the other half lives."

Not far behind the yellow convertible another car followed. Gabby Breen was behind the wheel and he chuckled softly to himself. He'd have the money first thing in the morning. Meanwhile, Chip Hilton wasn't getting out of his sight.

CHAPTER 6

ONE OF THE GANG

GABBY BREEN received his long-awaited letter early Monday morning and promptly at nine o'clock he shoved the cashier's check under the grill of the teller's window in the Parkville National Bank.

"Make it all fives," he said loftily.

The eyes of the teller behind the window opened wide in amazement as he scanned the piece of paper. "All five-dollar bills?" he echoed.

"That's what I said!"

"But—er—that will take considerable time, Mr. Breen, and I'm not sure we have that number of five-dollar bills available. May I have your identification?"

"Sure, take your time," Breen said carelessly. "S'pose I come back after lunch. Okay?"

The teller watched the flashily dressed man walk nonchalantly away from the window and out the door. "I think that fellow's a crook!" he muttered to himself. "I'd better have this double-checked!"

Breen was in a merry mood that Monday morning. He had the money now, and he wasn't worrying about Chip Hilton as long as he was in Eddie Duer's care, because he knew Duer was just as particular about his word as Stu Gardner. No, Duer wouldn't attempt to sign the kid so long as he was with the Bears. But that didn't mean Gabby Breen wasn't going to make hay while he had the chance. Meanwhile, he'd do a little scouting of the Bears and hope that the Mules lost the next three games. First thing on the docket, though, was to get acquainted with the kid chucker. "Sooner the better," he warned himself. "If I can sign Hilton, that Cohen kid will follow suit. I'd better use Corky to set Hilton up for a meeting. Gardner will probably beat it out of here and head for that hick town and wait for the kid to come home. Well, ole Gabby Breen will have Chip Hilton signed and sealed long before that."

Chip Hilton wasn't feeling so good that morning when he came down to breakfast. He was fighting the pangs of homesickness. But they were quickly dissipated when he saw Scissors Kildane waiting in the lobby. Kildane was standing by the desk and chatting with the clerk. When he saw Chip he came striding forward, the customary smile on his lips.

"Thought you were going to sleep all morning," Kildane chided good-naturedly. "You're in fast company, now, Chipper, and you have to get up early to be ahead of the pack. C'mon. I'll have a glass of milk while you eat your breakfast. Wouldn't be surprised if Duer has you throwin' for batting practice this morning. We hit at eleven and he wants you in uniform. In a Bear uniform!"

After breakfast Kildane drove swiftly to the ball park and ushered Chip into the clubhouse. He introduced him to the trainer, a cheery individual who greeted Scissors with a wide grin of affection and who gripped Chip's hand with a friendly pressure when they were introduced.

"Name's Potts, Hilton," he said warmly, "but the boys call me Pepper. You can do the same. Now, come on over here and let me get you an outfit."

The room was filled with Bear players, dressing slowly and idly kidding one another about their hitting, their weight, girls, and anything that came to mind. But there was an undercurrent of grim purpose in the room, and Chip sensed it was the stretch-drive pressure that was beginning to tell. The Bears had led the league since the opening week of the season, but the pressure had never let up; they could never seem to get a commanding lead.

After Chip was dressed in the Bears' home-field uniform, Kildane introduced him to every player in the room. Chip remembered some of them from the three games he had seen, but they looked entirely different close up. Mickey Curry, the powerful catcher with the long arms and the peg to the bases which had earned him the respect of every base runner in the league, was wholly different in appearance when you got next to him; his face was gentle, he spoke softly, and his smile was tender and friendly. Pete Mills, the lefty chucker who was tagged with the nickname "Windy," seemed to have the same personality off the field that he had in the box, and Chip knew why—the voluble chucker never stopped talking.

"This is Stretch Johnson, Chip," Kildane continued, "the best first baseman in the league."

The tall first sacker was about six-three and his arms seemed as long as Scissors' as he extended his hand, laughing and winking. "Kildane's a great kidder, Hilton," he said lightly. "Better watch him. He'll kid you right out of your shirt."

It was easy to see why Scissors Kildane was the most popular player on the Bear team. The big fellow always boosted his teammates, praised them all the time. Chip had only known Kildane a week, but he had never heard him make a derogatory remark about anyone during that time. He felt a surge of gratitude as he thought of the interest the tall pitcher had taken in him and, from the reception the tall chucker received from each player, it was apparent that Kildane was more than just a popular teammate to these men; he was a firm friend and their leader.

"Shake hands with Corky Squill, Chip. He's our lead-off hitter and the best in the business."

Chip had watched Squill work in the Mule games and he mentally agreed that Squill was a good second baseman. The keystone guardian didn't look five-nine, nor did he look as though he weighed a hundred and eighty pounds. Chip figured Corky Squill was the type of player who made enemies easily and liked it. He was quick-tempered, all right, and Chip had noted that Squill had been extremely careless with his spikes on the bases. Otherwise, Squill was a taciturn fellow, totally different from what one expected in a second baseman. Squill never said a word when he was on the field. Indeed, during the three games Chip had watched, the fellow had stood so quietly in his position and moved so imperceptibly that Chip couldn't figure how he managed to get into position to field the ball. But he did, every time.

"Glad to meet you, Hilton," Squill said briefly, extending a limp hand. As soon as Chip released his hand, Squill turned away.

Then Kildane introduced Coach Bob Reiter, Paul Hale, the third sacker, and the Bears' outfield guardians, Bill Dawson, Norman Klein, and Ted Smith. Their conversation was cut short when Eddie Duer called for the team's attention.

Chip studied the manager as he addressed his players. Eddie Duer was, Chip judged, about forty years old, six feet tall, and weighed about a hundred and eighty pounds. His movements were quick, and his steady black eyes were keen and bright. The prominent nose which had earned him the nickname of "Eagle Beak" was set above a small thin-lipped mouth, and his face was deeply tanned. Duer looked fit. His voice was sharp and he spoke decisively and forcefully.

"We've got to start hitting. We're getting the pitching, but we're going to run smack into trouble if we can't get more runs. We all know the pitching staff is overworked, but that can't be helped. Whitey's arm is in bad shape, and Scissors, Softy, Windy, and Phil just have to carry the load. They can do it, too, but they have to have some runs. The close ones are the killers. A pitcher can't let up; he has to bear down all the way.

"There's only two weeks to go, but the win-loss spread we've got isn't enough. The Mules are dangerous and we've got to face them eight more times. That means we've got to win from the rest of the league and hold our own with the Mules. Now, I want you fellows to keep in mind that the next two weeks mean everything; every game is important, and every hit and every throw's vital. And I want you pitchers to keep in mind that every batter you face is up there ready to knock the bread off your table every time he looks at the apple. We're at the turn, now, and it's up to us to set the pace."

Duer paused and nodded in Chip's direction. "I guess most of you have met the kid who won the most valuable player award in the high school tournament, but I want to welcome him officially and let him know that as long as he is with us he will be considered a member of the team and treated like a player. Hilton, I know the boys join me in welcoming you as one of the gang—" There was a burst of applause and then Duer continued.

"Now let's go out and get some more hitting. Hilton, you can throw a few soon as you loosen up."

Chip's heart was jumping as he warmed up, and when he walked out beside the mound and started pouring his control pitch across the plate he was shaking as if from the ague. This was something. . . . He was serving them up for regular professional players in a regular ball park. But Chip didn't try anything fancy— didn't fog his fast one across the plate—he simply concentrated upon his control, placing the ball where the hitters could meet it solidly.

Up in the stands, Gabby Breen was seated in the same seat he had occupied for the past week and some of his friendly Bear fans were there, too. Breen was watching the tall towhead whip the ball effortlessly across the plate and he was pointing out the important pitching traits Chip possessed.

"Watch that pivot! Smooth, eh? You can tell a real chucker by his pivot and his stride. The kid's got a nice, easy stride and a perfect finish."

"You must like him," someone said meaningly.

"I do and I don't," Breen said appraisingly. "Lots of kids have form, but they gotta have that fast one and the change-up and good control to get anywhere in the big time."

"Looks like a *great* prospect to me," a fan said firmly. "He showed a lot of stuff setting those kids on their ears last Sat'day."

"Yeah," another fan added, "didn't give a hit in eighteen innings. Personally, I wouldn't waste any time signing that kid."

Breen didn't do much talking after the game started. He was thinking about the package locked up in the hotel safe, and his approach to Chip Hilton. But he managed to do considerable scouting of the Bears. Breen figured he'd need a lot of help if he got Boots Rines' job; have to win from the Bears above all.

He smiled as he thought of his conversation with Hoot Kearns. Come this time next week he might be managing the Mules. What a break! Of course Boots had given him a job when he needed it and had helped him out on a number of deals. But baseball was like any other business and a fellow couldn't let sentiment enter into it. Boots hadn't delivered, and if he lost out, it was his own fault. Boots was a chump. He should've signed the guys Kearns wanted. Then it would have been the boss's responsibility. Well, *he* wouldn't make that mistake, once he got to be the big wheel.

Breen glanced at Squill. He would need Corky. That is, if he got to be the manager of the Mules. He focused his eyes on the chunky infielder. He'd taught that kid a lot, corrected his faults, and got him into pro ball.

Even after Squill had made the grade with Parkville, Breen had worked with him, made suggestions concerning his play, and given the aggressive little infielder inside tips.

Breen's forehead wrinkled suddenly and two deep frown lines formed between his eyebrows and his close-set eyes narrowed as he watched Squill's immobile figure. "That's it," he muttered, "that's it! Now to go to work on him."

The Bears had an easy time that afternoon. Scissors Kildane was ahead of the Panthers all the way and the Parkville fans were thrilled as their idols chalked up another win, 7 to 1. Chip was thrilled, too. He was getting his first introduction to inside professional baseball. Eddie Duer told him about the signs between the catcher and the keystone combination.

"Curry gives the signs, Chip, and, unless the pitcher shakes him off, Corky and Bucky flash 'em on to the rest of the team. That way, every player on the field knows what pitch is coming and knows just about where a batted ball should go. Signs aren't infallible, of course. Especially if the hitter's timing is bad, if he swings too early or too late or checks his swing or changes his stance—why, the ball may not go where we expect it —but at least knowing the kind of a pitch helps us anticipate the probable direction the ball may take if hit."

Duer explained, too, that the Bears used three sets of signs and that they were changed frequently, sometimes in the same game. "Lots of coaches can steal a team's signs and we have to be careful," he added.

The Bears didn't need their last licks and Chip waited for Scissors after the third out in the top of the ninth. Eddie Duer waited, too.

"That's it, Scissors," Duer said decisively. "That's all the chucking you're doing for another week. You, my long-legged friend, are going to take a rest!"

"A rest?"

"That's what I said. A rest! We're going to need you going down the stretch and you're takin' a little vacation."

"You mean I'm leaving the team?"

"No, nothing like that, but you're leaving the pitching to the rest of the guys for a week. Same thing!"

Kildane shook his head obstinately. "Nothing doing. I'm taking my turn. I don't need a rest."

"I say you need a rest and that's that!" Duer said firmly. "Now, you beat it!"

Kildane accepted the manager's decision without

further argument, but he wasn't sold on the idea. "Don't understand it," he said lamely. "I never felt better in my life. Guess Eddie knows what he's doing, all right, but I'd rather take my turn. Heck, I got a rubber arm. I could pitch every day."

Stu Gardner was waiting at the hotel when Kildane and Chip arrived and the scout joined them at dinner. He confided that he was leaving town and told Chip that he probably would see him the following spring at State.

"You'll like it up there, Chip," he said enthusiastically. "It's a great institution and you're lucky to have the opportunity to further your education there. By the way, don't let anyone talk you out of your decision to go to college, no matter how attractive the proposition. Remember, you'll still have the same opportunity when you finish your college studies and you'll be a better pitcher. Am I right, Scissors?"

Kildane nodded soberly. "He sure is, Chip. I wish someone like Stu, here, had talked to me when I dropped out of high school. My coach and the folks tried to get me to stay in school, but like most kids I thought I knew it all. Yep, Stu's plenty right, Chip. You'll have lots of time to play ball after you get that sheepskin. I didn't get many offers, but you'll sure be getting them, Chip. And they'll be hard to turn down —some of them."

"There's no doubt about that," Gardner agreed. "Some people will tell a kid anything to get him signed to a contract. What's more, they'll offer you cold cash out of all proportion to what you think you're worth. In a case like yours, Chip, unscrupulous men often try to tell you that it's all right to sign a contract and accept a cash bonus and then go on to college and play ball. A fellow would know that wasn't right if he took time to think it over, but operators like that don't give you a chance. No, there's nothing right about signing a big-league contract and then going on to college and keeping it secret and pretending to be an amateur. A boy who signs a baseball contract becomes a professional as soon as he signs, and all the talk in the world won't change the fact.

"Well, I've overstayed my time. I've got to be in Cleveland tomorrow morning and that's a long drive. I'll be rooting you in, Scissors. Take good care of Chip, here. S'long."

Chip and Kildane stood at the curb a long time after Gardner's car had disappeared, and then headed for a movie theater. As they walked along they talked about the friendly scout. Both agreed that Stu Gardner was a square shooter and a fine man.

Gabby Breen had observed the meeting between Gardner and the two pitchers and he kept them in view all through the meal. After dinner he followed Chip and Kildane as far as the movie theater and then set out to meet Corky Squill. Thirty minutes later Breen and Squill were seated in the scout's car on a country road a few miles out of Parkville. Gabby Breen well knew the league rules about interclub fraternizing and so did Corky Squill. That was the reason they were so cautious in concealing their meetings.

"Hear anything about the Hilton kid? Going with the team?" Breen asked.

"Sure. He's goin' with us."

"S'pose Duer's signed him?"

"Nope, I don't think so. He's goin' to college, the way I hear it."

Breen smiled grimly. He'd have something to say about that. After he'd pressured the kid and his mother with all that dough.

"Maybe Duer's got him already signed," Breen ventured, watching Squill covertly.

"You don't know Eddie," Squill said dryly. "Duer's got principles. He said he wouldn't try to sign any of those kids and he meant it."

Breen changed the subject. "I hear you and Eddie ain't been hittin' it off too good," he suggested.

"Aw, we get along good enough. Except when he starts gripin' when I throw the spikes a little. Heck with that!"

Breen nodded. "Right! Corky, I've got news for you. Boots is on his way out."

Squill was incredulous. "What's that? After winnin' the pennant last year? And fightin' down the stretch right now? You're nuts!"

Breen shook his head in mock sympathy for Rines. "Poor guy," he sighed. "They been on him heavy. They're sore 'cause we can't knock you guys off. You know how they hate to lose to Parkville."

Squill chuckled mirthlessly. "I know," he said grimly. "No doubt about that. We just own you guys, that's all."

"Funny," Breen mused, "on paper we're tops—pitching, hitting, and fielding. Can't figure it."

"Maybe Eddie owns Boots," Squill said dryly. "Ever think of that?"

The darkness hid Breen's twisted smile. "What do *you* think?" he queried. Without waiting for a reply, he continued, "Sure, I've thought of that! So has the front office! Listen, Corky, we got three games before we take you guys on in Hedgetown. Two with the Lions and one with the Panthers. And if Boots doesn't win those three games the wolves up in Hedgetown will tear the park down. Another thing, if Boots goes, Gabby Breen moves in."

Breen sat back, smirking and basking luxuriously in the personal gratification his words suggested.

"You mean as manager?"

"That's right! Sure as we're sittin' here. Kearns told me that over the phone last night."

There was a deep silence as Squill thought about Breen's statement. Then Gabby threw another bombshell.

"You wanta pick up three, four thousand bucks for doin' nothin'?"

Squill grunted incredulously. "Huh! What do you think? How?"

"Easy. Just by arrangin' a meeting with me and that Hilton kid and helpin' to get his moniker on a contract."

"How could I do that?"

"Easy. All you gotta do is play up to him. Only you gotta work fast. Okay?"

"It's a deal. I can sure try."

Gabby Breen extended his hand. "Okay," he said. "It's a deal! Shake!"

There was another brief silence, each man busy with his own thoughts. Then Breen nudged Squill with his elbow.

"I can't wait until tomorrow, Corky. Brother, if I get to be the boss of the Mules, you're comin' with me as my team captain, sure as shootin'."

"Heck, Gabby, what makes you think Duer would sell any of us guys? You're nuts!"

"Yeah? Not so nuts! Especially if the Mules win the pennant. Heck, I'll be able to buy any player I want."

"How the Mules gonna win?"

"By winning five of the eight with the Bears. Look, I got it all figured. S'pose the Mules lose the next three. That leaves 'em with twelve games to play, and eight of them games is with the Bears. See? And if the Mules can win five of the games with the Bears, they're in. They'll win the pennant and Gabby Breen will be in solid as the manager of the Mules and there will be a big bonus and he'll have full say on replacements and the first one will be one Corky Squill as team captain and a big increase in salary. That bad?"

An ugly expression spread across Squill's face and his black eyes glittered dangerously. For a second his whole being expressed so much pent-up rage that Breen instinctively moved away. Then Corky recovered his self-possession and sank back. But his words rang just as dangerously.

"Look, Gabby, if you think I'm gonna get out of line for you or for anyone else you're crazy. Why I oughta hang one on your chin for—"

Breen's voice was silky and smooth as he checked the excited second baseman. "I'm not askin' you to get out of line, Corky, in any manner or form. Look, maybe I'm countin' too far ahead, but I just wanted to cut you in on any good luck that might be comin' my way on this deal. Heck, maybe nothin' at all will happen."

Breen paused and then continued with studied care. "They're a pretty good bunch to work for, the Mules. Hoot Kearns is a great guy and the Hedgetown fans can't be beat. Why, they gave some of the guys houses when they won the pennant last year. They'd go for you in a big way.

"I didn't mean you had to do anything wrong. You play your best all the time. Nothin' wrong so long as you can do that, is there? Only thing is, I gotta sell you to Kearns as a holler guy, as a leader and a hustler and that means you gotta change your style of play in the field. I'll give you the dope on that later. Right now, my big interest is young Hilton."

CHAPTER 7

SHORT CUT TO FAME

CHIP was surprised the next morning when he appeared in the Bear dressing room, for Corky Squill was the first player to greet him. "Hiya, Chip," Squill said pleasantly. "You know, yesterday when you was chuckin' was the first time I've had a good hittin' workout all year. I sure wish you was goin' to be with us all the way. Sure you can't make it until the end of the season?"

Chip warmed to the belligerent little infielder immediately. "No, Mr. Squill," he said, "I've got to—"

"Name's Corky," Squill growled good-naturedly, a wide grin on his face. "You call me Corky."

"All right, Corky," Chip said awkwardly. "If you'd like, I'll throw some more to you this morning. That is, if Mr. Duer wants me to."

"He'll want you to all right," Squill said, grinning.

Minutes later Chip and Squill walked out to the field together and began warming up. Squill was greatly pleased with himself. He could almost feel that three-thousand-dollar roll in his pocket. "Duck soup," he muttered. "Gabby will pull that suitcase trick and this kid will fall like a ton of bricks." Then Squill's face

70

clouded—Gabby had signed him up for a measly three hundred bucks.

Corky Squill didn't know the half of it. Breen had sold Squill's contract outright to Malloy and the Bears for a flat ten thousand dollars. Squill didn't know that, of course, but the doughty second baseman knew the fast-talking scout hadn't given him a very good deal. Corky had always felt that he should have received a bonus when he joined the Bears. But Corky was grateful for Breen's interest because he had been just a green kid when the wily scout signed him up. That was Breen's *modus operandi,* he signed up every kid in sight, played the field, and hoped one of the lot would click.

Before Chip walked out to the box to throw for batting practice, he and Squill were on friendly terms. Corky could be extremely likable when he had the desire, and money was the incentive to which the keystone guardian responded most quickly. Corky wanted that three thousand dollars and meant to get it. He invited Chip to be his guest for the evening and chuckled gleefully to himself when the invitation was accepted.

"We'll take in a show and talk some baseball," Corky said enthusiastically. "Okay?"

In the dugout, when the game started, Chip found himself beside Scissors Kildane. The lanky chucker was complaining, good-naturedly, but still enough to show he didn't like being pampered. His conversation was directed toward Chip but was loud enough for Duer to hear.

"Won't even let me throw in the bull pen," Scissors grumbled. "Must be out of his mind. I gotta throw every day. I got that kind of an arm. Heck, we're in the stretch. I wanta play!"

If Eddie Duer heard Kildane he gave no indication. But he showed he knew what he was doing that afternoon, Scissors or no, for Windy Mills was as fit as a fiddle. The talkative chucker limited the Wasps to three hits. At bat the Bears were murderous. They chased three Wasp hurlers, and fattened up their averages by amassing a total of eighteen hits. The game was a 13–0 rout.

The Bears' afternoon was made a complete success by the Lions. All through the game the Bear players and fans watched the pitchers' duel which was indicated in the Mules–Lion game by the long rows of zeros on the scoreboard. But in the last of the ninth, the Lion frame showed up with a big three and brought a cheer from almost every person in the park.

Gabby Breen nearly cheered, too, nearly gave himself away, barely refraining from joining in the exulting roar. But he caught himself and limited his pleasure to a satisfied chuckle. After the first joyous cheer, Breen's grandstand seatmates began needling the Mule scout.

"Looks like you guys will be lucky to end up in third place," someone chided.

"Public School Six could beat the Lions," another fan added.

"Hey, Breen! Hey, Gabby!" a shrill voice piped. "You better get yourself a uniform. The Mules are fallin' apart!"

Breen grinned and took the razzing in stride. The fans weren't making him mad by celebrating the Mules defeat. Gabby was doing a little mental celebrating of his own. Two to go, and maybe he *would* be wearing a uniform . . . a uniform as the manager of the Mules.

Squill joined Chip and Kildane at dinner that evening and surprised both by his gaiety. Kildane had never seen his teammate in such exuberant spirits. Long after Chip and Corky left for the show, he was still trying to puzzle it out. Although Squill was highly regarded for his all-around baseball skill, his taciturnity had provided a barrier beyond which few of his teammates cared to venture. The lone exception was Stretch Johnson, the Bears' big lefty first baseman. Corky and Stretch were two of a kind, quiet, self-contained, and closemouthed. The similarity of their dispositions probably was the reason for their friendship. At any rate, Stretch Johnson was the only Bear regular Corky Squill cared two hoots about.

Corky bought the theater tickets, overruling Chip's objections, but good-naturedly agreed to let his companion buy the milk shakes after the show. They were scarcely seated, however, when Corky excused himself.

"Shucks, Chip, I forgot to check with Pepper. Got to let him know where we're goin', you know. One of Duer's trainin' ideas. I'd better call him! Be right back!"

Corky's fertile mind had manufactured that excuse on the spur of the moment. He wanted to call Gabby Breen and let him know the progress he was making with Chip Hilton. Breen was waiting for the call and was just as excited as Squill.

"Gabby? . . . Corky! Guess what? . . . Right! . . . Right with me! And that ain't all. Now listen! The kid's plannin' to go home tomorrow and get some clothes and stuff and meet us again at Clearview. You better manage to bump into us tonight, somewhere. . . . Tony's Chop House? . . . Right! Around ten."

Gabby Breen was whistling softly to himself when he finished his telephone conversation with Squill. And he continued to whistle as he made his plans. Gabby had decided that Chip Hilton would have company when he went home the next day. When he bumped into them in Tony's Chop House one would have thought Corky Squill and Chip Hilton were the last persons in the world Breen expected to see.

"Hey, Corky! What are you doin' here?"

Squill's act was perfect, too. Obviously he hadn't seen Gabby Breen in years.

"Gabby!" Squill exploded. "Why you old son of a gun! Come on, sit down. Oh, by the way, this is Chip. Chip Hilton."

Breen evidenced surprise but he didn't overplay his act. He gripped Chip's hand hard and looked the youngster up and down with approving eyes.

"You look bigger out there on the field. Saw you pitch the championship game. Congratulations!"

"Won the most valuable player award, too," Squill said proudly.

Breen nodded. "Couldn't miss," he said. "Had to be, had to be."

The conversation swung away from Chip, then, much to his relief, and the next half hour was devoted to the Midwestern League race and especially to the Bears and the Mules. Squill and Breen batted the ball back and forth and Chip listened. While he listened, he appraised the flashy scout, studied the pasty face and the shifty eyes. In spite of Chip's attempts to close his mind to the thought, he couldn't keep from thinking that Gabby Breen was a perfect example of the kind of baseball scout Stu Gardner had described as designing and irresponsible. But Chip tried to be a pleasant companion and concealed his dislike for the loquacious scout as best he could.

Just before they left the restaurant, Squill mentioned that Chip was going home in the morning to pick up some clothes.

"That's a coincidence," Breen said, laughing. "I'm going right through Valley Falls on my way to Hedgetown. I can drop you off."

Suddenly Stu Gardner's warning came back strong to Chip. He didn't want to be obligated to the flashy scout, but he couldn't compete with both of them, and, in the end, reluctantly accepted Breen's invitation.

Breen beamed. "We'll leave first thing in the mornin', Chip. I'll pick you up at the hotel at eight o'clock."

The four-hundred-mile drive passed pleasantly. Breen was talkative enough to make Chip feel at ease, and thoughtful enough to turn on the radio after lunch to the broadcast of the Mule–Lion game at Clearview. A strange feeling gripped Chip, then, and for the first time he realized that Gabby Breen and Corky Squill had violated the fraternizing code Stu Gardner had told him about.

Players, managers, and scouts were forbidden to fraternize and he had been a party to the violation scarcely a day after Gardner had explained the ruling.

The Mules were having trouble with the Lions and the game went into extra innings. Breen was driving steadily, absorbed in the game, and Chip's thoughts had free reign. He was sorry now that he had accepted the ride. Still, Corky Squill had been so nice that it would have been embarrassing to refuse.

The Lions won the game 2 to 1 when the travelers were a short distance from Valley Falls, and Gabby Breen's impetuous grunt of pleasure caught Chip by surprise. But the wily scout quickly covered up.

"Looks like the Bears are going to back in, Chip, if we keep losing. Even if the Bears did drop one to the Wasps today at Parkville."

"I guess every game's important now," Chip ventured.

"They sure are. If the Bears knock us off next Saturday and Sunday they'll just about knock us out of the race. By the way, Chip, are you interested in professional baseball?"

Chip shook his head. "No, Mr. Breen, not now. I'm planning on going to college."

"Takes money to go to college."

"It sure does. I don't know whether I'll be able to make it or not, but I'm going to try."

"You know, Chip, I may be able to help you out. Of course I can't talk about that until you get home. What time does your mother get home from work?"

Chip explained that his mother was a telephone supervisor and wouldn't be home until eleven o'clock. "She doesn't know I'm coming home tonight. Guess I'll surprise her."

Gabby Breen decided that he'd surprise Mary Hilton that night, too. "I'll have to work this clever," he was thinking. "The suitcase deal ought to be just the ticket. This kid doesn't want his mother to work and I'll play that up strong, too. Maybe I'd better use the association gag since this kid is so set on going to college."

A few minutes later they were in Valley Falls, and, despite Chip's protest, Breen insisted on driving him home.

"I may not see you for a few days, Chip, but sometime soon I'd like to see your mother and talk to her about your future. Think it would be all right if I dropped around to see her in a week or so?"

Chip hesitated for a brief second and then assured Breen it would be all right. But after the scout left, Chip berated himself for being such a softy. "I should have told him it was no use," he muttered.

Breen checked in at the Valley Hotel and spent the rest of the evening making his plans and arranging the money in the suitcase. He debated a long while upon the amount he should place in the bag and finally decided upon half the amount—five thousand dollars. "That ought to do it," he soliloquized. "Then I'll give Corky three thousand and put the other two grand in the old sock. Not a bad night's work."

At eleven o'clock Breen sighed "at last" and picked up the suitcase. Ten minutes later he rang the Hilton doorbell.

Mary Hilton looked at Chip questioningly. "Now who could that be at this late hour?"

"Probably Soapy," Chip said as he hurried to the door. He was surprised to find Gabby Breen, but he recovered quickly and asked the scout into the house.

"Mother, this is Mr. Breen, the gentleman who drove me home today."

Breen acknowledged the introduction, and then answered the unspoken question he saw in Chip's eyes. "Had trouble with my car right after I left, Chip. Just got it back. In a way I'm glad I had the trouble, though. You see, I work on the side for an important baseball organization and they contacted me at the hotel. And you know what? They told me to stay right here, and see you, Mrs. Hilton."

Mary Hilton was confused. She gazed at the flashily dressed stranger questioningly as Breen continued:

"Your son is a fine athlete, Mrs. Hilton, and the organization I represent is deeply interested in his future. It's our business to protect youngsters like him from unscrupulous talent scouts and fly-by-night promoters. That's why I'm here. My boss received a number of reports on William, especially, since he won the most valuable player award up at Parkville, and Chip is his Number One player. The Number One player in the whole country, in fact. He insisted that I talk to you while I was here.

"Baseball is big business and every kid is entitled to

the best proposition he can get. That's where this organization I represent comes in. The Baseball Protection Assurance Association specializes in protecting talented youngsters from big and small baseball interests that try to exploit them.

"We've enrolled hundreds of boys in our association and no youngster has ever regretted joining up. Of course every boy is checked and rechecked and screened until we *know* he's a sure-fire big-leaguer. We don't approach a boy unless we're sure of that."

While the visitor was talking, Chip was studying the card Breen had handed him and trying to figure out what this visit was all about. The card was neat and businesslike, but the name of the association was unfamiliar. Chip was confused. Nothing he had learned from Stu Gardner seemed to cover this situation.

"Since we are not affiliated with the big leagues nor any other baseball organization," Breen continued, "salary contracts, bonus agreements, and all of the usual big-league restrictions do not apply to our association. There's no obligation on your part, as William's mother, Mrs. Hilton, nor on your son's part. There are no dues, no fees, and no contract to sign. Simply an application for membership in the association.

"And as soon as it's signed you and your boy will get a cash bonus! And there's no strings on the money. You keep it, no matter if the association never gets Chip a contract with a big-league organization!

"It's my guess that William, here, will be signed up inside of six months to a big-league contract and that the cash bonus at that time will be no less than *twenty-five thousand dollars!*

"That ain't hay, and all but twenty-five hundred of that will be yours. You'll get twenty-two thousand, five hundred dollars in addition to the cash bonus you get as soon as you and William sign the association application."

Mary Hilton was just as confused as Chip, but the personal responsibility of keeping her little family going had given her an insight into practical business. "How does the association benefit?" she asked. "How can it afford to do all this?"

"Well, it's privately endowed for one thing," Breen explained, "and its operating expenses are partly covered by the ten per cent of the bonus money a boy may receive when and if he's signed on with a big-league organization. Then the ten per cent is fed right back into the association to keep the organization going and to help some other worthy boy. You see, the president of our association is a wealthy baseball fan, and he's interested in kids. He wants to see them get a fair deal. That's why he founded the association. In fact, he endowed it with his personal fortune."

Breen turned to Chip. "Well, youngster," he said lightly, "what do *you* think about our association? Got any questions?"

Chip shook his head. "No," he said uncertainly, "I don't think so. Only I want to go to college. That is, I've been planning on it."

"Fine," Breen said briskly. "Doesn't mean a thing! You can go to college if you wish and you get the money just the same. Furthermore, you'll get a hundred dollars a month all the time you're in college. That would pay a lot of those college expenses and there's nothing wrong with it. It isn't like signing a big-league contract."

Breen nudged the suitcase with his knee and covertly studied the faces of his bewildered listeners. Then he made his decision. Rising suddenly, he grasped the suitcase and startled Chip and Mary Hilton by lifting the wide-opened valise above his head to send a shower of five-dollars bills downward, covering the buff-colored living room rug with a carpet of green.

There was a stunned silence. Chip looked at the hundreds of bills in amazed incredulity. Mary Hilton's gray eyes were wide with shocked fascination. With a flourish, Breen drew a paper from his pocket and forced it into Chip's hands.

"There you are, son," he said pompously, "there's your money! *Five thousand dollars!* Just sign the application and pick up all those five-dollar bills! They're all yours!"

Chip forced his eyes away from the pile of bills to the paper he was holding. He had never seen so much money in his life. Why, five thousand dollars would pay off the mortgage on the house. Pay it in full. And if Breen got him a big-league contract, why he'd get another bonus and his mother could stop working . . . forever!

He opened the paper and looked questioningly at his mother. Mary Hilton was still overwhelmed by the sight of the money on the floor. She was completely bewildered by the sudden display of wealth. Chip's heart overflowed completely then, love for his mother filling his chest with an almost unbearable pain and choking off his speech completely. He pretended to read the words on the paper but his eyes were blurred by deep emotion and he couldn't see a thing.

Then Breen made a mistake. He mistook Chip's intense quietness for indecision. Thrusting a pen into Chip's hand, Breen pointed to the signature line at the bottom of the page.

"Sign right there, boy," he said brusquely. "Remember, you're leaving for Clearview tomorrow. You ought to be in bed. Besides, you've got to talk to your mother about your college plans."

Thirty minutes later Gabby Breen headed back toward the Valley Hotel. Beside him, on the seat of the car, he clutched the bag with nervous fingers and shook his head unbelievingly. His lips kept forming bitter self-accusing words. "Where did I slip up? It always worked before! What went wrong?"

Chip could have answered those questions. Breen's big mistake had been his reference to college. All of Chip's dreams, and the hopes his mother had so often expressed, had flooded his thoughts, then, completely drowning out the money appeal. Then, too, he had recognized Breen's scheme for the subterfuge it was. And the words Coach Rockwell had drummed into his mind come rushing back. "An education is an asset which a fellow can never dissipate; no one can take it away from him! Money and friends may vanish, but an education sticks forever!"

So Chip had told Breen he would not sign the application until he had talked it over with his coach. The boy's quiet refusal had startled Breen, and he had spent many anxious minutes trying to convince Chip and Mary Hilton how foolish it was to turn down such an opportunity.

"Why, you're sure to get a big-league bonus of twenty-five thousand dollars and you'll have a salary besides," Breen had argued. "How can you give up all that money? Show me the college graduate who can trade a diploma for twenty-seven thousand, five hundred dollars! And a salary, too?"

Chip hadn't said so in so many words, but that was one of the things which had convinced him that the proposition was wrong. Stu Gardner had told him that a boy who was being paid because of his baseball prowess was a professional, whether or not he waited until after he was graduated from college to play professional ball.

Breen had tried every way he knew to shake the boy's decision but Chip had been adamant. In his heart Breen knew he had lost out on the youngster, but he kept trying. He finally persuaded Chip to promise to give him a final answer Saturday when he came to Hedgetown with the Bears to play the Mules, and then he had put on his hat and left.

Long after Chip had fallen asleep, Mary Hilton sat thinking about her son and the problems he was now facing and would have to face in later years. And she was happy because Chip had shown that he could make his own decisions. Happy, too, that he had not been swept off his feet. Chip had demonstrated that he was intelligent enough to consider important matters carefully and sensible enough to seek advice from responsible persons before rushing impetuously into an important situation. But she was proudest of all because Chip had proved that he was big enough to turn away from a tempting short cut to fame and fortune.

CHAPTER 8

PENNANT TENSION

HENRY ROCKWELL leaned back in the big easy chair in
his front parlor and stroked the wide armrest with both
hands as he listened to Chip's story. His black eyes reflected pleasure when Chip had finished the story and
the words he spoke reflected his elation.

"Good! Good for you, Chipper! I think the fellow's
an outright faker! I never heard of the Baseball Protection Assurance Association! Sounds fishy to me! No
legitimate baseball operator would approach a high
school boy with a proposition like that.

"The fact that this man offered you bonus money
stamps his association, whatever it's called, as a subterfuge—a stunt to get around the rules applying to boys
who want to keep their amateur standing. Tell you
what you do. When you meet up with him in Hedgetown, suggest that he make an appointment with me to
talk about the proposition. Okay? Mark my words, he'll
never show up. I'd bet my life on that."

An hour later Biggie Cohen, Speed Morris, Red
Schwartz, and Soapy Smith listened to the story while
Speed's jalopy chugged toward Clearview. And each
agreed wholeheartedly with Rockwell's conclusion.

"The Rock can spot a faker a mile," Schwartz declared. "If he says this Breen is pulling a fast one, you can bet he's right."

"Stu Gardner tipped us off on his kind," Biggie added.

Speed Morris changed the subject. "What about this Scissors Kildane, Chip?" he asked. "Is he as good as the papers say?"

"Better!" Chip declared. "He's got everything, a fast ball, a knuckler, and a hook that breaks a mile."

"Bears gonna win?" Schwartz queried.

Chip got started on the Bears then, and he was still praising them when they pulled up at the Clearview ball park. It took him only a few minutes to get passes for his friends and hustle into his uniform.

Corky Squill had been watching the players' gate all through the pepper game and warm-up. When Chip came out on the field and headed for the dugout, Corky sauntered over for a drink of water. "Hiya, Chip," he said pleasantly. "Glad you're back. We missed you."

Scissors Kildane came charging up in time to hear Squill's words. "That's right, kid," he said. "We missed you for batting practice. Eddie wants you to throw again today if your arm's okay."

Squill hung around, eager to pump Chip to find out if Breen had made a deal. He was thinking about the three thousand dollars and was on pins and needles. When Kildane joined the pepper game, he moved close to Chip and lowered his voice. "Breen drive you up?" he asked softly.

Chip shook his head. "No. I came up with friends."

"He took you home, didn't he?"

"Oh, yes, but then he went on to Hedgetown. Or at least that's where he said he was going."

"He talk to your folks?"

Chip was surprised at the turn of the conversation,

and surprised by Corky's curious interest. "Yes," he said thoughtfully. "Mr. Breen talked to my mother."

Squill waited expectantly, his quick black eyes suddenly sharp and penetrating.

"And?" he said.

"Why, that's about all."

The bell and Eddie Duer saved Chip then, the bell sending the Bears out on the field for batting practice and Duer waving Chip to the mound.

Squill was disappointed. He hadn't learned a thing and his anxiety increased. Maybe the kid had been signed up by the Drakes all along. Gabby had been worried about Stu Gardner and his friendliness with Duer. Corky glanced sourly at Duer. "Maybe Eddie's in on it, too," he muttered. "I wouldn't put it past him."

Chip lobbed the ball straight over the plate for each hitter the first time around, gradually increasing his speed, but putting the ball where the hitters liked it each time. Pregame hitting is designed to sharpen the hitter's timing, not to prepare him for tricky pitching.

Duer named Phil Akers to start for the Bears. The tall two-hundred-and-twenty pounder had been used all year as a relief pitcher but the temporary shelving of Kildane had forced Duer to assign him to a starting role. Akers was fast but wild, and his erratic throwing kept the Bears in hot water all afternoon. The Lions, fighting desperately to hold their position at the top of the second division and taking full advantage of Akers' wildness, got out in front 2 to 0 in the first, and didn't need their ninth-inning time at bat to win, 8 to 3.

Chip took the defeat as hard as the Bear players. He had wanted his Valley Falls buddies to see the league leaders at their best. Corky Squill had been the biggest disappointment. The stocky keystone guardian had a miserable day in the field, booting three chances and going none for four at bat. The strength of any baseball team is down the middle, from the catcher to the pitcher, the second baseman and the center fielder. That line of strength was weakened by Akers' wildness and Squill's errors, and that was the difference.

After the game the Valley Falls contingent headed for the hotel, and Chip joined Kildane for dinner and a show. Corky Squill retired in sullen silence to his room, angry with himself for his bad day and barely able to restrain his impatience as he waited for Gabby Breen's call.

As the hours wore on, Squill's anxiety increased and he paced the floor impatiently. At nine o'clock the call came and Squill had the receiver to his ear before the first ring ended. But he got little information. Gabby Breen was a careful man. He wasn't going to hold a lengthy conversation over the telephone, and Squill agreed to meet him at a motel on the edge of town.

Corky Squill was a cautious fellow, too. He wasn't going to take any chances with the league's fraternizing rule. Eddie Duer was an extremist where the league rules were concerned and demanded that his players follow them to a letter. Duer wouldn't even permit his Bear players to talk to those of another club off the field. "You can nod to 'em," he would warn, "but that's all. No conversations and no friendship stuff! You pal up with your own teammates!"

Corky took a taxi and alighted a short distance away from Breen's cottage. Making sure he was unobserved, Squill knocked on the door. Inside, without a word of greeting, he plunged right into the subject which had been disturbing him all day.

"What happened?" Squill demanded. "I couldn't get a thing out of Hilton."

Breen's pasty face flushed red. "I couldn't either," he

admitted sourly. "Gardner must have him signed up. The kid claims he isn't and that he won't sign until he gets out of college. Tried to feed me a lot of bunk about ethics and professionalism."

"What about the dough? How about the suitcase trick?"

"Didn't work. Something's wrong, though. His mother has to work and they've got a mortgage on the house and they're as poor as church mice. I can't figure it out."

"That kid's smooth," Squill said thoughtfully. "I bet the Drakes got him tied up."

Breen shrugged his shoulders and flattened his hands in a gesture of disgust. "Forget it," he said bitterly. "We've got other things to think about. Guess you know the Lions took us for two and that means Boots is on his last legs. I'm high-tailin' it into Hedgetown early in the morning because if the Panthers take us tomorrow it'll be smart for me to be around when Kearns starts squawkin'. Now listen, if Kearns fires Rines, I'll be in charge of the Mules for the Bear game Saturday afternoon sure as shootin', and that's why we gotta get together. Right?"

Squill said reluctantly, "I guess so, but I don't see where I come in."

"You come in as my field captain next year, that's where you come in! But I can't wait until next year to sell you to Kearns. I wanta sell him on you right now, the very first day I'm in charge of the Bears. Get it?"

Squill nodded dubiously. Breen was too fast for Corky, too clever with words and ideas.

"You see," Breen continued, "the minute Kearns appoints me manager I'm gonna start talkin' about next year and I'm gonna tell him you're the guy we need to give us the pennant. Only, as I said before, I gotta sell

Kearns on the idea you're a hustler, a pepperbox, a fighter, and a real leader. And that means you gotta go back to your old style in the field. Think of it, you'll get a big jump in salary and be the captain of the Mules and workin' with me."

Squill was visibly impressed. This was the out he had wanted, the chance he had dreamed about. He hated Eddie Duer because the leader of the Bears made him walk a straight line and toe the mark on and off the field. His thoughts went winging into the future.

"But you're the one who changed my style of play," Squill replied, puzzled. "You told me to change. You never told me why, but you said I moved around too much. I don't get it!"

Breen's lips tightened in a mirthless grin. "You don't have to get it. You just do as I say and start it in the Bear practice tomorrow. All I want you to do is go back to the original style. Now listen!

"You guys will get to Hedgetown about nine o'clock," Breen said glibly, "and you can reach me at this telephone number. Now, you call me just as soon as you get in town. If the Mules lose tomorrow, kid, I'll have some good news for both of us and you'll be on your way to some real dough."

Eddie Duer didn't believe in letting a league-leading team take it easy, or get the notion they were good and thus fall victim to overconfidence. Now that the Bears had lost two straight games to second-division teams, he was all the more determined to insist on the off-day practice the next morning. Chip and Scissors were among the first to be dressed and out on the field. Duer was talking to Mickey Curry and greeted them with a quick smile.

"No throwing for you today, Chip," Duer said. "Every

other day will be enough. Today you chase some flies, take a turn at bat, and generally take it easy."

"What some managers won't do to impress a ball-player," Scissors wisecracked.

"You mean till they get 'em signed," Curry quipped. "The guy *never* gives *me* any rest."

On his way to the outfield, Chip trotted past Corky Squill and called cheerily. "I'm backin' you up, Corky. Don't worry about a thing."

Squill deliberately turned his back and pretended he had not heard Chip. But the slight was obvious and Chip was disturbed.

Corky was sore, all right. He was sure Chip had lied to Breen about wanting to finish college before signing a pro contract. Bitterness filled his thoughts and his resentment toward Chip increased as he thought about the three thousand dollars which had flown out the window.

Eddie Duer was no help. In fact, Duer added fuel to the flame of Squill's anger by directing his biting criticism toward the second sacker. The aggressive manager wasn't going to overlook Squill's sloppy play of the previous day. Duer didn't bypass the rest of the club, though, and went right down the line, giving each a bit of a dressing down. But he concentrated chiefly upon the infielders, drilling them again and again on double-play combinations and plays to the plate. The entire pitching staff chased flies in the outfield. Kildane, Richards, Mills, Akers, Burns, Goodman, and Falls were hustling as much as the outfielders. Chip took his turn, too, thrilled by the opportunity to pull in a long fly from the bat of Ketch Kerrigan. Kerrigan was the strongest man on the squad and could hit the ball a mile. Duer used him as a clutch pinch hitter and the big fellow invariably came through.

After a full hour of fielding, Duer was satisfied. There was an expression of satisfaction on the manager's face when he assembled the squad at home plate, but he wasn't through. The crafty manager realized his young club had reached the crucial point of the campaign, the point where pennant tension had begun to tell. This team could lose its poise and its effectiveness overnight. The coming two-game series with the Mules probably would tell the story. Duer's pleased expression masked the keen appraisal he made of each player as he talked.

"We've been sloppy on the bases and we've slipped up on a couple signs when it hurt. Slapping fines on a player who boots a sign doesn't help anyone, and I've tried to avoid the practice. But there's no excuse for missing a sign when all a fellow has to do is step out of the box or call for a repeat if he's on base.

"So we'll just spend half an hour reviewing the signs. Let me have the regular batting order and you pitchers man the bases. Chip, you used to work behind the bat, s'pose you handle the plate."

"Me, I wanta play first!" Kildane chortled. "Come on, gang. We'll show 'em some classy infieldin'!"

Windy Mills winked at Stuffy Goodman as the two lefties wheeled about and dashed for shortstop and second base respectively. Boiler Burns trotted down to the hot corner. Richards, Akers, and Falls headed for the outfield. Chip started the ball around the horn and, after it made the rounds, tossed it to Duer. For thirty minutes the hard-working manager called the situations, gave the signs, and then fungoed the ball while the regulars ran the plays. Not a sign was missed.

"Nice goin'!" Duer said, calling them to the plate once more. "Now we'll have a couple of races and finish up with some hitting. First, we'll take the infielders. Line up at the grandstand and finish at second base.

Bob, you start 'em and I'll clock the winners. Chip, you run with the chuckers."

Corky Squill was by far the fastest infielder on the team and won easily. Surprising enough, Stretch Johnson came in second. The tall first sacker took tremendous strides but couldn't overcome Squill's fast start. Bill Dawson, the speedy left fielder, won over Norman Klein by a stride in the outfielder's race, and Chip led the pitchers all the way, winning by five yards. Windy Mills and Scissors Kildane matched stride for stride until the very end when Mills forged ahead.

"All right," Duer shouted. "All first and second place winners. A new glove for the champ. Line 'em up, Bob."

"I'm betting on Hilton!" Kildane shouted. "Dinner and the works! Any takers?"

"Against the field?" Whitey Falls demanded.

"Sure!"

"It's a deal!"

"You're making a mistake, Scissors," Chip protested. "You'd better not."

"I already have," Kildane retorted. "Get on your horse, kid!"

"Okay, guys, let's go," Bob Reiter said briskly. "Line up as I call your names. Johnson, Klein, Dawson, Mills, Hilton, and Squill. Now each of you fellers take hold of the wire there on the grandstand and don't let go until I reach the count of three. Got it? Okay. On your mark, now! Hold that wire! Get set! One—two—three!"

Corky Squill was the only runner who tried to beat the count, breaking on Reiter's "Two!" The split-second advantage shot him three strides ahead. Chip broke a little late, but when he sped past the catcher's plate, he was only a yard behind Corky. Chip could tell from the yelling that the race was between him and Squill, and he really began to pump.

"Come on, Chip, you've got him," Kildane roared.

Halfway to the pitcher's mound, Chip pulled even with the speeding infielder and forged ahead. Then before he could lengthen out his long legs he felt a vicious jab in the ribs and broke stride, almost falling. As he tried to regain his timing he heard Squill's mocking laugh and saw the fleet infielder spurt out in front. Even as he stumbled, Chip could hardly believe it, could hardly believe Corky would do a thing like that. But it was true and Chip knew it. Corky Squill had elbowed him intentionally. Chip tried to figure out the reason as he dug his spikes desperately into the turf.

"Foul!" Kildane shouted. "Foul!"

Chip wasn't finished. He had been through the mill in broken-field running with a football under his arm and had mastered the knack of regaining his balance quickly. Now he churned his feet until he was almost upright and then dug after Klein, who had edged ahead and was now second to Squill. Corky thought he was in, let up a little, and made the mistake of looking back. He couldn't believe his eyes. Chip had regained his stride, had passed Klein, and was only a yard behind. Almost before Corky could jerk his head back, Chip was alongside. The two straining figures held even for a second, but only for a second as Chip's long strides ate up the distance and drew him steadily ahead. He held his pace to cross the finish line a yard ahead of Squill.

Chip heard Kildane's triumphant shout as he eased off and slowed down to a slow trot. Then someone grabbed him by the arm and jerked him around. It was Squill and his features were distorted with rage.

"What's the idea of elbowin' me?" Corky demanded. "That the kind of a guy you are?"

Chip stared at Squill in astonishment. He was caught

by surprise, left speechless. "Why, I never elbowed you, Corky—"

Squill flung Chip's arm roughly aside. "Don't give me that stuff!"

Scissors Kildane came swinging up, his pleasant features unusually sober. "I saw it, Corky," he said quietly. "You did the elbowing. You owe Chip an apology."

Squill's face purpled. "Me apologize?" he yelled. "Me apologize to that punk? Nuts! Nuts to you and him, too!"

"That will be enough, Corky," Eddie Duer said harshly. "We all saw it. Now drop it! Chip won and you lost and that's all there is to it. All right, everyone, that's all!"

But it wasn't all and every person on the field knew it. Corky Squill was a hard loser and the incident wasn't closed by a long shot. Chip Hilton had incurred the enmity of the taciturn infielder and that meant trouble for the kid chucker and for Scissors Kildane and the whole club. It might even mean the pennant.

CHAPTER 9

FEEDING THE WOLVES

GABBY BREEN was an experienced motorist and had spent most of his adult life behind the wheel of an automobile. But he was a careless driver and his handling of a car usually reflected his moods. This particular morning he was in a hurry, as full of tension as an electric cable. This time tomorrow he might be the boss of the Mules.

The flashy scout decided to check in at the Mule office just before game time that afternoon, and when he reached his room in the motel he dressed carefully for the meeting he had planned with Hoot Kearns. Sighing regretfully, he selected a blue gabardine suit, black shoes, and gray hat. A plain white shirt supplanted his favorite pink silk and a solid maroon tie completed his attire.

Breen liked the brilliant shades but this was an important day in his life, his first big break, and Gabby didn't intend to bobble the opportunity. He appraised himself in the mirror. Not bad," he mumbled. "Makes me look kinda dignified. Maybe I ought to go in for this straight stuff all the time."

Breen knew that he was wishful thinking. He was

happy only when his flamboyant personality could have free play and be set off by colorful attire. He sat down at the small desk and rehearsed his plans for the day. First, he'd make the rounds and feel the pulse, so to speak, of Hedgetown's baseball fans. He'd hit the hotel first, and then the drugstore, and the big cigar store on the corner. Then he'd drop into the sports shop, the newspaper office, the poolroom and the bowling alley.

"That ought to do it," he reflected. "Hmmmm, Gabby Breen, the manager of the Mules. Now, let's see, everyone knows me as Gabby but that don't click with the job. I gotta get some sort of a manager's moniker like the Silver Fox or the Master Mind or Mister Baseball or something real fancy."

Breen was still thinking about that when he finished his tour of Hedgetown's baseball centers and sauntered into Hoot Kearns' private office.

Kearns was in a bad mood. The present Mule losing streak had just about knocked his team out of the pennant race and the Hedgetown fans were loud and bitter in their criticism of Boots Rines. Kearns liked the tall, easygoing manager and had stuck by him through all the weeks of criticism. But baseball is a business and the harassed owner of the Mules had let sentiment sway him beyond the bounds of good judgment. Baseball fans paid the salaries of players and managers and the Hedgetown rooters had begun to use the weapon which hurts most—the empty seat. Yes, the Hedgetown fans had practically deserted the identical team which had won the championship a short year before. Kearns knew a drastic change was imperative. He glanced up impatiently.

"Hello, Gabby. Been expecting you. What's new?"

"Nothing much, boss, except that I've got some bad

news. Just couldn't sign that kid, no way," Breen replied. "Here's your ten thousand," he added, as he handed Kearns a cashier's check from the Valley Falls National Bank.

Kearns motioned to a chair beside the desk. "Sit down, Gabby. What happened?"

"Well, just like I told you over the phone, I drove him home and sounded him out and figured my angle. Seems the kid's father is dead and they're pretty hard up. Anyway, I pulled all the stops and thought I had him on the ropes, but he stuck to the college idea. I think Gardner's got the kid tied up."

Kearns shook his head. "No, Gabby, you're wrong. I've known Stu Gardner a long time. He wouldn't sign up a kid who wanted to play college ball. He's not the type."

"Could be," Breen said reluctantly.

Kearns' voice had a slight edge when he continued. "Never mind that, Gabby. There's more important work to be done right now. Guess you've seen the papers.

"Seems like every person in town is down on Boots. They even blame him now, when the Bears win from the Panthers. If we lose today, we're practically out of the race and I'll have to make some sort of a move or that ball park will be empty the rest of the season. You prepared to take over if a change has to be made?"

Breen didn't answer immediately. He gave the appearance of weighing the proposition carefully and reluctantly. "I guess I'm prepared, all right, Mr. Kearns," he said thoughtfully. "Of course I don't feel too good about Boots, but I guess someone has to take over, and if you want me—"

"I wouldn't ask you if I didn't want you," Kearns said shortly. "Suppose we leave it this way— If the Panthers take us this afternoon, Boots is out and you're in. Okay?"

Breen nodded, and it was all he could do to veil the exultation which flooded his eyes. It would be okay, all right. And the Panthers' Number One fan this afternoon would be Gabby Breen.

Kearns swung around in his chair and switched on the radio. "Might as well sit in on the game," he said with a half-smile. "First time I ever let the results of a game over the air influence my selection of a manager."

During the next hour and thirty minutes Gabby Breen gave Hoot Kearns a first-hand demonstration of his acting ability. He moaned and groaned through every inning as the Panthers piled it on the faltering Mules.

Hoot Kearns gave up in the sixth when the Panthers went out in front 11 to 2, absent-mindedly listening to the game as he debated his managerial crisis. At any rate, the dropping of Boots Rines would appease the wolves until the end of this season. Then he began to evaluate Breen, wondering if he wasn't making a mistake. But he knew the flashy scout was popular with the fans and with the baseball writers and he hoped he might serve as a temporary tonic for the whole organization, perhaps give the players enough of a lift to pull them out of their slump.

When the last Mule hitter struck out in the top of the ninth, Kearns stretched out his hand and grasped the hand of his new manager.

"You take charge first thing in the morning, Gabby," he said decisively. "We've lost three straight, so it isn't a bad spot for you. The law of averages ought to start working right about now and maybe you'll get off on the right foot. I guess I don't have to tell you how much these two home games with the Bears mean. If we can win both we'll still be in the race. Well, good luck! You'll need it!"

Breen's heart was thumping with excitement. "Thanks, Mr. Kearns," he managed. "Don't worry about these two games. We're goin' to take 'em both! I know what I'm talkin' about!"

"I sure hope so," Kearns said ruefully. "Oh, by the way, keep your mouth tight about Boots. I want to let Rines know about the change first, before I release it to the papers. I hate to feed Boots to the wolves, but it's the only out I have. The deadline on the morning paper is midnight and after that you'll be the new manager of the Mules. S'pose you meet me here tomorrow morning at nine o'clock. I'll call a meeting for ten o'clock and turn the team over to you at that time.

"Oh, yes, you'd better be lining up your pitching plans. Murph will help if you wish. He knows exactly how we stack up as of this minute. Turner worked today, as you know, and Baker pitched Wednesday. That means that anyone else you want to use tomorrow ought to be okay. See you in the morning."

Breen's mind was working feverishly. Now to see Corky. It was a good thing he had told Squill to call him tonight.

Beatrice Dobson, Kearns' secretary, never even glanced up when Breen left the office but kept her green eyes glued to the work on her desk. Two sharp buzzes signified that Kearns wanted her, so she gathered up her pad and pencil and walked just a little too briskly into the inner office, her leather heels clicking defiantly upon the hard floor.

Kearns was a discerning man and he knew his secretary's moods. She was displeased about something and he knew exactly what had affected her. But he gave no sign, spoke in a soft voice, and told her to have the club secretary draw up a new contract for George Breen who would manage the Mules for the duration of the season.

Miss Dobson sniffed audibly and bore down so heavily on her pencil that the point snapped. "Darn," she said disgustedly. "Nothing seems to be going right around here!"

Kearns grinned slightly. "Having trouble?" he asked.

"Not half the trouble you're going to have with your new manager," she said, walking briskly from the office.

Kearns pondered Miss Dobson's words as the pencil sharpener in the outer office whirred angrily in protest to the secretary's vigorous cranking. Somehow or other he had experienced the same feeling every time he had considered Breen for Rines' job. He shook his head forebodingly. Beatrice Dobson was psychic or something when it came to analyzing people and it was fairly obvious that one George "Gabby" Breen had been given an extremely low rating. He sighed and reflected that it was too late now. It was done and he'd have to hope for the best.

Kearns would have been shocked had he been able to read Beatrice Dobson's thoughts. She was hoping for anything but the best where Mr. George Breen was concerned. She considered him a self-centered individual who possessed none of the elements of leadership required of a baseball manager and, furthermore and definitely, she knew him to be an absolutely uncouth and disagreeable person.

Meanwhile, the Bears were on their way to Hedgetown. Bus rides seemed to relax the players and they usually behaved like a group of kids out for a picnic. But not this time. The two defeats and the afternoon's unpleasantness had left a tension in the squad which an ordinary bus ride couldn't erase. Eddie Duer sat beside Chip most of the trip and talked to him about his pitching. The husky manager was fond of Chip and determined that the boy should get more than a vacation out of the trip. The bus ride gave him the first real opportunity to talk intimately to the kid chucker.

"Chip," Duer said pleasantly, "you're with us for one reason and one reason only—because you were a unanimous selection as the most valuable player in the tournament. No person in our organization will try to influence you to sign a contract at any time. Stu Gardner happens to be one of my best friends and he told me all about your plans for a college education. I'm all for that! After your college career is finished, the Bears will be tickled to death to have you with us for a year or two before you go up to the big time. But we have no other plans with respect to your future. Understand?"

Chip nodded. "I sure do, Mr. Duer, and I appreciate it a lot."

"And," Duer continued, "while you're with us, we want to help you with your pitching. So, if you have no objections, one of us will talk to you every day. I'm taking the lead-off position because I'm the top man. First, I s'pose we ought to start with your delivery.

"Guess you won't mind a few criticisms, especially when they're for your own good. Now, for one thing, you don't conceal the ball. You see, the more you can hide the ball from the hitters, the less chance they have to focus on it and get set. Some pitchers show the ball to the batter several times and then hide it at the last second. Other chuckers *never* show the ball to the hitter, keep it hidden in their gloves and behind their legs and bodies until it seems to come out of nowhere.

"Other fellows let you see the ball when they start their deliveries and then hide it until it suddenly pops over the plate. You should make up your mind on a certain kind of delivery and then stick to it. Another thing, you've got to learn to use the same delivery for every pitch. Every pitch must look alike so far as your delivery is concerned. Get it? Good! Now, I'll let Curry work on you."

Duer stood up in the aisle and called to the burly catcher. "Hey! Mickey! Wanta talk to Hilton?"

Curry swung around in his seat and nodded his head. "Sure," he boomed. "I wanta tell him how to keep runners from gettin' too big a lead." He looked significantly at Windy Mills as he lumbered down the aisle.

Mills grunted. "Huh! Catchers with bum arms always blame the pitchers."

"Some pitchers I know ought to go back to high school and get a little coaching," the popular captain murmured.

Curry seemed to overflow into the aisle and against Chip when he sat down. The big catcher was built like a bulldozer and his arm was the talk of the league. The ball was just a flash of light between the plate and the bases when he tried to catch a runner and there wasn't a Bear infielder who didn't complain about the heavy ball the burly receiver threw. He nudged Chip with his hard right arm.

"You've got a lot of stuff, kid, a lot of stuff. A year with us and you'd be ready for the big show. I don't know what Eddie Duer told you, but I'll just talk about pitchin' in general and maybe you'll get something out of it.

"There's all kinds of pitchers, Chip. Some are temperamental, some are mean, and some are pleasant and easygoin' like Scissors. You're a lot like Scissors, if you don't mind me saying it. You've both got a lot of speed and a slider and a change-up and you've both got control. What's more important, you're hard workers and team players.

"Kildane's the answer to a manager's prayer, Chip. You know why? No? Well, I'll tell you. He's one of those rubber-arm guys who want to do all the pitching. If he had his way, he'd chuck every day. You know, he'd be priceless as a bull-pen fireman, as a relief chucker. Fact is, Eddie uses him like that now, almost, and that's why this bunch of kids are winning. We all know that. Heck, Kildane's the difference. We'd be just another young ball club, 'cept for me, of course, if it wasn't for Scissors. Most chuckers have to have their rest—but not Scissors! All he needs is a yawn and he's ready!

"Today's baseball is power-hitting baseball and every manager in the game is looking for the guys who can knock the apple out of the park. But there isn't a manager in baseball who doesn't know that you have to have top pitching and a reliable relief chucker or two in the bull pen if you're going to be leading the pack in September. That's why Scissors has meant so much to us. Every time one of the other guys gets in a jam, Scissors is on Eddie to put him in to put out the fire. Maybe I'm talking too much about the big bean pole, but all I can say is he's one of the best in the business, and if you pattern yourself after Scissors Kildane you'll be headin' in the right direction."

Curry talked to Chip all the way into Hedgetown but the rest of the players were unusually quiet. Most of the Bears were trying to catch up on their sleep. All except Corky Squill. Corky was sitting in the rear of the bus, sulking and thinking about Chip Hilton and Eddie

Duer. At that moment he hated one just about as much as the other.

Corky Squill was the sort of fellow his nickname implied, the kind of ballplayer who seemed always to bob up at the right time and in the right place. But he hadn't always been like that. In fact, Squill probably would have remained a small-time semipro if it hadn't been for Gabby Breen.

Several years earlier, when Squill was eighteen, Gabby Breen had signed Corky to a contract. Gabby didn't believe Squill was going anywhere but he had signed him as a matter of course. The following spring, one of Breen's many ventures included the assembling of a team for a small-town promoter who was operating on a shoestring and Squill joined the squad. Breen stuck around long enough to get the shoestring and the team. It wasn't much of an outfit, but it was good enough for the local competition, and, to pass the time, Gabby really coached. He held field practices twice daily and skull practices at night. After a month, however, the venture folded and Gabby released the players. But during that month he had worked seriously with the only halfway ballplayer on the team—Corky Squill.

Corky had only one fault as an infielder, but it was a serious one. It was a fault that, if uncorrected, would keep him from ever getting anywhere in professional baseball. He telegraphed the catcher's signals by his very actions on the diamond. A batter had only to watch the excitable second baseman to know what kind of ball was coming up to the plate next. Breen set himself the task of breaking the exuberant Corky of his playing habits at second base.

Squill had been a miniature Breen in those days,

loudmouthed, showy in dress and in behavior on and off the field. And Gabby Breen was his hero. Corky aped everything the flashy manager did, his speech, his dress, and his actions. It was not surprising, therefore, that he followed Breen's orders to the letter. Breen had changed Corky's style of play and also his cocky deportment. So much so, in fact, that Corky became just the opposite of his former self. At the start, Squill had caught the fancy of the local fans because of his holler-guy attributes and Gabby Breen couldn't stand that kind of competition. Gabby had to be the center of attraction when it came to showmanship. So he had stepped on Corky, checked his talk and his extravagant gestures in the field and at bat.

Almost overnight, it seemed, Corky Squill developed into a closemouthed, silent individual, who concentrated solely upon fielding, throwing, and hitting. He steeled himself to such an extent that he became an automatic machine in the field, silent of voice and free of motion until the ball came his way. He never again, by his actions, telegraphed a pitch or a play. Corky had never gotten away from that training, had acted out his artificial being just because Gabby Breen had said that was the type of ballplayer he should become if he was to make good in pro ball. This on-the-field behavior had carried over into his general personality until he became morose and moody. His Bear teammates had tried to loosen Corky up but had found him impossible. Now they accepted him as he preferred to be, silent and efficient, a lone wolf.

Squill was glad when the bus rolled into Hedgetown. First, because he wanted to find out how Breen had made out with respect to the managing job, and second, because he was disgusted with all the attention Chip Hilton was receiving. But, silent as he had been on the bus, he couldn't resist a contemptuous barb in Duer's direction when they unloaded in front of the hotel.

"Two in a row to the two weakest teams in the league," Corky said bitterly. "What is this? Bush league baseball? Sand-lot stuff? We gonna kick away the pennant just because of a lot of high school malarky?"

Eddie Duer wheeled about and grasped Squill by the arm. "That'll be enough, Corky," he said coolly. "We didn't lose those two games because of the tournament."

"How about the bench rule?" Corky demanded belligerently. "How about an outsider in the dugout? Any ballplayer knows an outsider in the dugout is a jinx!"

"That remark will cost you exactly fifty dollars," Duer said grimly. "You see me in my room at eight o'clock sharp. Understand?"

Squill shrugged his shoulders contemptuously and turned away. There was an awkward silence as the other players ignored the incident and busied themselves with their baggage. Chip's face was blazing and he tried his best to pretend that he hadn't heard Squill's remarks, but every word had burned itself into his heart. He lugged his bag into the lobby and sank down into a chair. So that was it! Corky Squill thought Chip Hilton was an outsider and a jinx.

CHAPTER 10

ICE WATER IN HIS VEINS

EDDIE DUER had been in baseball a long time. First as a minor-league player, later as a scrappy infielder in the big leagues, then back to the minors, finally emerging as a successful manager for the Drake chain. Duer had been a tremendous success with the Parkville club. The fans liked him and Duer had the complete confidence of the owners. Duer realized his job's multiple objectives and worked hard at developing young players and at the important task of making the team carry its own weight, pay its own way. A winning club is usually a paying club, but Duer had proved that a team could be popular as long as it was a hustling club and played heads-up ball. Duer had well earned his success, working hard with his young players and at the job of pleasing the fans. Because his success had never gone to his head, never elevated him to the point where he thought he was invaluable, he became more than a successful baseball manager in the eyes of the Parkville citizens; he became one of them, one of their own.

Duer was supremely happy in his job and in Parkville, and he was proud of his team. After all, they were chiefly kids. Now, as he sat in his room waiting for

Corky Squill, he was thinking about the youngsters, the rookies who had made such a gallant showing. He checked each one, right through the batting order.

Corky Squill, the lead-off hitter, had what it took to be a real ballplayer, all right; that is, if you could divorce him from his surly disposition. He was fast, possessed a good arm, and played to win. He was usually ahead of the play in his mind and seldom failed to make the right move. As a lead-off man he was ideal, worked the pitcher into a hole more frequently than not, got on one way or another, and was smart and fast on the base paths. Furthermore, he hit a consistent .300. But he was antagonistic and temperamental, a slave to the traits which had spoiled the careers of hundreds of big-league prospects.

"Why can't he be like Bucky?" Duer murmured. "What in the world's wrong with the guy?"

Bucky Boyd, the other kid member of the keystone double-play combination, was exactly the opposite from Corky Squill in every way except physical make-up. Bucky was the holler guy of the team, a hustler in every situation, and as pleasant as they came. He was a great "push-along" batter, a master of the drag bunt, and as fast as a streak.

The Number Three hitter, Bill Dawson, covered left field like a blanket, had a good arm, was fast, and hit a solid .290 from the first-base side of the plate.

"Bill's goin' places," Duer muttered. "Nice kid!"

The cleanup spot was filled by Stretch Johnson. The big fellow hit and threw lefty, and he was considered the best first sacker in the league.

"In his second year, too," Duer said enthusiastically, nodding toward the empty chair facing him and thinking of the big awkward kid who had tripped over every blade of grass in Bear Stadium's outfield until he had worked the kid out at first base. Duer chuckled. "Even fooled me, the way he came along."

The smile was still hovering on Duer's lips as he thought of his other regulars. Shifting to the outfield for his fifth and sixth hitters he thought about Norman Klein and Ted Smith. Klein was one of those big fellows who seemed to smell a hit coming before the batter tagged the ball, made the catch look easy. He hit the long ball and he made a hit with every fan and teammate because of his hustle and friendliness.

Smith was a rookie, playing his first professional baseball, but he played right field like a veteran. The tall kid could make the long throws and was hitting like a fiend.

"Over his head, maybe," Duer solemnly assured the chair, "but he's bound to be called up next year or the year after."

Duer's eyes glistened when he thought of his seventh hitter. Hale was everyone's favorite. The third baseman looked like a high school freshman with his blond, crew-cut hair and his kewpie-doll face. But he didn't handle the hot corner like a freshman. The kid threw the ball on a string and ate up everything which came his way.

"Isn't bad with the stick, either," Duer confided to the chair. "All I need is one more year with that baby and he'll be ready. Gotta give Mickey a lot of credit, though. He knew what was what when he said Pauly belonged on third."

That brought Duer to Mickey Curry, the workhorse catcher of the Bears. The burly field captain worked behind the plate day after day and it was Mickey's leadership almost as much as his own, Duer thought happily, which held the kids together. He'd have been lost without Mickey.

Duer leaned forward, his words barely audible. "You know," he whispered, "Mickey's the best thing ever happened to me and Parkville. He's *made* baseball in this town." Duer leaned back in his chair, thinking about his best friend.

Mickey Curry could have gone up to the Drakes a dozen times but he wouldn't leave Duer and Parkville. "Me," the human bulldozer would growl pleasantly, "I'm a small-town boy. I like the sticks. Besides, the Drakes already got a coupla catchers. And I like to play every day."

Duer relaxed comfortably in his chair and began thinking about his pitching staff. But the thoughts weren't good and little by little he straightened up. Kildane was overworked, fine as a razor, badly in need of a rest. If he could only get by these next two games with the Mules he could rest Scissors up for the key games down the stretch. But who could he use? The last two games had been disastrous. Richards had come down with a bad arm in the second game with the Wasps, and Akers' erratic pitching at Clearview yesterday had given the Lions the 8–3 victory. Forgetting Whitey Falls and Stuffy Goodman, who were nursing bad arms, that left Windy Mills and Boiler Burns and the Mules "owned" them both.

"It all adds up to Scissors," he said bitterly, "just as it has all year. Maybe I could try Softy tomorrow. . . . No, he's almost as fine as Scissors and the Mules love cute stuff. I'd better hold him for Sun—"

Duer's one-way conversation was interrupted by a knock on the door. It was Corky Squill. Squill had heard the murmur of Duer's words and was surprised to find the manager alone.

"Sit down, Corky," Duer said pleasantly. "You fellows have got me talking to myself."

Duer studied Squill's sullen face until the second sacker was seated and then continued, his voice gentle and persuasive. "You were off base this afternoon, Corky, 'way off. I hated to slap that fine on you, but you left me no choice. What's the trouble?"

"Plenty!" Squill said shortly, his black eyes glittering angrily. "What is this, a ball club or a baseball school for high school hot-shots?"

Duer's placid features tightened and his jaw line bulged, but he restrained the impulse to answer Squill with angry words. Not all the strain in a tight baseball race is borne by the players. The manager's burden is a heavy one and every decision down the stretch becomes momentous. Eddie Duer was a fighter, quick, intent, and sure of himself. Yet he was an extremely friendly person. But pennant tension gets into the blood of everyone connected with a pennant contender and does something to them, changes their very natures until the pressure is off. Squill's contemptuous attitude and biting words struck fire, sent a burst of rage coursing through Duer's whole body. It required every last ounce of his self-control to restrain the angry words which sprang to his lips. But he forced them back and managed to speak calmly.

"First and last, Corky, the Bears are a baseball club. A good one. Your job is to play ball the best you know how and to follow the orders of the manager. My job is to run the ball club and co-operate with the management. It seems to me that you are forgetting that your job has nothing to do with promotions or general policies or with managing the club."

"What about the playin' field? On the field?"

"I don't quite understand what you're getting at but as a player your job is chiefly concerned with playing ball."

"And how about the dugout?"

"You have your player rights there, too."

"Well, as a player tryin' to win the pennant, ain't I got any right to beef when you let a smart kid jinx the club by sittin' down there on the bench smirkin' and actin' like a big shot—"

Duer rose to his feet. The muscles of his face were contracted and his complexion was fiery red but his voice remained calm.

"That's enough, Squill. Before you came up here I had hoped we could iron out the matter on a friendly basis, forget the fine, start all over. But you're impossible. So far out of line I can only take recourse to authority and disciplinary measures—

"Now you get this! You play ball and keep your mouth shut about the high school tournament and about strangers on the bench and about Chip Hilton! Or—Buddy Coons takes over at second base and stays there whether we win the pennant or not! Got it? Furthermore, this afternoon's fine stands and I'm slapping another one on you for tonight's insubordination! Good night!"

Corky Squill backed out of Duer's room and went slowly down the hall. But he didn't go to his room. Corky was boiling. His whole being was filled with hate for Eddie Duer and the kid he blamed for all his trouble, Chip Hilton. He left the hotel and hurried along the streets until he came to a drugstore. Inside, he waited impatiently until he could gain a telephone booth. And while he waited, his furious mind tried to devise some way to get even with his two self-styled enemies. He'd call Gabby. At least Gabby was the kind of man you could talk to. Maybe it was fraternizing, but the heck with it! Anyway, he wanted to know how Gabby was making out with the manager's job. Duer couldn't do any more than he was doing already . . . taking all his pay . . . and threatening to replace him with Buddy Coons. Heck, Coons couldn't carry his spikes! Yet, Duer was a stubborn guy, you had to hand him that, especially when he was hot under the collar. Maybe he'd better play it smart and play ball and wait for a chance later to get even. Heck, he might spoil his whole career if Duer benched him now. Best thing he could do was to play ball the way Gabby wanted him to play and hope Hoot Kearns would be impressed. It was gonna be tough being a holler guy when he didn't feel it, though.

While Corky Squill was waiting for a chance to get into a telephone booth, Gabby Breen was striding up and down in his room impatiently waiting for Squill's call. Squill was vital in Breen's plans, now, and he was worried sick that the little second sacker might not call him.

Breen liked to stay at the Circus Drive-In Court because it was out of the way and he could be sure of peace and quiet. But every little sound irked him as he waited and he kept glancing at his watch. At nine-thirty the phone in the one-room cottage rang. It was Squill.

"We're in, Corky!" Breen shouted gleefully. "I've got the job! Start in the mornin'! How's that for good news?"

Squill was doubtful. "Funny," he said questioningly, "we got in before supper and no one said anything about it."

"No one knows it," Breen said exuberantly. "Come on out! Hurry! We're on our way to big dough, kid!"

Chip joined Kildane at the breakfast table the next morning and right away he sensed that something had happened. He glanced around quickly. All the players were talking animatedly. Kildane shoved a newspaper toward him.

"Read the headline, Chip," he said pointedly.

Chip glanced down and almost jumped. He understood what had caused the interest now, all right. Then he turned back to the story.

BOOTS RINES RESIGNS AS MANAGER OF MULES

GABBY BREEN TAKES CHARGE TODAY

H. B. Kearns announced exclusively to the *Courier* last night that Frank Rines had submitted his resignation as manager of the Hedgetown Mules to take effect immediately. Kearns stated that the resignation had been accepted and that George "Gabby" Breen, the popular Mule scout, would assume charge beginning with today's game with the Bears. It has been evident for some time that a change was imperative and the *Courier* wishes to assure the fans of the city that it is strongly behind the change.

BREEN IN TIGHT SPOT

The new manager, Gabby Breen, takes charge of a team, which, on paper, is the strongest member of the Midwestern League. Yet, the Mules have played second fiddle to the Parkville Bears all season, showing no evidence of the fire and effectiveness which carried them to the pennant last year. Loss of the two-day series which opens here this afternoon will be disastrous, since the locals trail the Bears five games in the win column and have dropped four more in the all-important loss column. Breen was not available for comment when this paper went to press, but the *Courier* joins Hedgetown's fans in wishing the new manager good luck.

"What do you think of that?" Kildane demanded.

Chip shook his head. "I don't know," he said slowly. "I didn't get to know Mr. Breen very well."

"Just as well," Kildane said shortly. "He's a bad egg. Can't understand why they'd choose him over Rines, but it's none of my business. I know one thing for sure. We can look for some fast stuff now."

"You mean bench jockeying?"

"Right! Trouble on the field, too! At least Breen's got that kind of reputation. Well, we'll see."

Kildane saw, all right, and so did Chip. Breen started what he had termed his "aggressive baseball" with the first pitch that Red Willis, the Mules' big lefty, threw to Bucky Boyd. Squill had flied out to right field and when Bucky strolled up to the plate it seemed an invitation for the Mules to start what was to be an exciting afternoon. Catcalls, hoots, and then a pitch which headed straight for Boyd's head and which the shortstop evaded only by a miracle. Chip felt sure Willis had thrown an intentional duster. And, as the game continued, he had no reason to change his mind. Willis' apparent wildness was effective, for the Bears went down one, two, three.

During the warm-up practice, Scissors had tried to inveigle Duer into letting him pitch, had used every argument, but the manager had made up his mind to go with Windy Mills. That was a mistake. The big lefty was strong and fast enough, but he had no control where the Mules were concerned. They "owned" him. Not so much because they could hit against him, but because they could upset him. A little bench jockeying from the Mule dugout went a long way with Mills. Boots Rines had controlled it to a certain extent, but there was no control today. It was Gabby Breen himself who took the lead. And that was all the Mules and the Hedgetown fans needed.

Mills' unsteadiness seemed to spread to the whole club. Corky Squill even seemed jittery. At least Chip thought so. For the first time since he had seen Squill play, the keystone guardian seemed full of pep. He was on the move constantly, immediately after the signs and before and after each pitch. Furthermore, he had suddenly become a holler guy, yelling and pepping it up to the surprise of everyone.

Chip couldn't understand the sudden change in Squill. Scissors had said Corky had ice water in his veins. Well, it must have come to a sudden boil. The Bears' keystone guardian acted as though he had run into a hornet's nest. Chip concentrated on the Bear second sacker. Something had happened to the Corky Squill he had come to know.

CHAPTER 11

SOPHOMORE ROOKIE

SCISSORS KILDANE was the toast of the Midwestern League but he was just a kid, what you might call a second-year rookie. Most observers forgot that the tall, poised chucker who had carved out a record of twenty and four in his rookie year and who had won thirty and lost but six so far in his sophomore year of professional baseball was just old enough to vote. That was because his natural co-ordination and pitching know-how on the diamond gave you the impression you were watching an experienced veteran. But under the Bear cap and uniform, Scissors Kildane was an unspoiled, overgrown kid with a lot of the old college try and spirit who had proved he was no sophomore flop. That was why he suffered agony every time a hit rang off the Mule bats.

Kildane was going with Windy Mills on every pitch and, from his vantage point in the bull pen, his eyes

116

kept shifting from the mound to the dugout, searching for Eddie Duer and wondering why the peppery little manager didn't call him to come in and put out the fire. The Mules went out in front 3 to 0 before the Bears could retire the side. At that, it needed a sparkling 6–4–3 double play, Boyd to Squill to Stretch Johnson with three aboard, to save Mills from an avalanche. The top of the second brought up the Bears' long-ball hitters, Johnson, Klein, and Smith, but Red Willis wasn't letting anyone take a toe hold at the plate, dusting them back with just enough wildness to be effective and once again it was one, two, three for the Bears.

Something happened to the Hedgetown fans, then, and whatever it was it transformed each and every one of them into a miniature Gabby Breen. At least Chip thought so. He had never seen such a sight. Red Willis, bat trailing in the dust, stalked out to bat. Pandemonium broke loose. The Mule dugout was alive with jumping jacks all screaming and yelling at Windy Mills, while Gabby Breen in the third-base coaching box and the coach at first base seemed to go into hysterics. Then the fans went on a throwing spree, sending a shower of paper cups, hot dogs, and crackerjack boxes flying to the accompaniment of their frenzied cheers. Chip held his hands over his ears and leaned forward to watch the effect upon Mills. He was glad *he* wasn't out there in the middle of all that confusion and bedlam.

Before the game, in the dressing room under the stands, Kildane had sauntered over to Duer and told the manager that he felt like a million, and hoped he'd have the chance to put the Mules where they belonged —in the second division. But Duer had brushed him off, telling him that he was resting out the series.

"But I'm right, Eddie," Kildane had protested. "This is one of the big ones to win. Let me get it for you!"

Kildane was talking in vain. Duer had made up his mind and sent the tall chucker out to the bull pen. "Not today, Scissors," he said kindly. "Maybe tomorrow."

When the Bears took the field for the bottom of the second, the telephone in the bull pen jangled and Kildane dove for the receiver. "Here I go!" he quipped.

But Kildane was wrong. Duer wanted Burns to warm up. Boiler Burns was a control pitcher and Duer figured he might still the Mule bats after Mills' wildness. But he was still hoping Mills might settle down.

"It's you, Boiler," Kildane said, turning to the husky chucker. "Eddie says you're next."

Kerrigan, the big pinch hitter who doubled as a relief catcher and outfielder, stood up and punched the catcher's glove. "Come on, Boiler. Let's get those guys."

"Sure hope Windy settles down," Burns grunted. "These guys murder soft stuff in this ball park. Scissors is the only chucker we got who can handcuff 'em in this joint."

"It's sure funny," Kerrigan said. "Windy's fast ball usually works against them at home."

But Mills didn't settle down. Before Burns had cast a dozen worried glances in the direction of the mound, Windy had passed Willis and Butch Bates, the Mules' lead-off hitter, and Duer had called "time." But Duer didn't take Mills out of the game. He sent the rangy pitcher out to left field and waved Bill Dawson out of the game. Dawson trotted back to the bull pen and sat down.

"Here we go," Dawson said fearfully. "Eddie's goin' to try Boiler, and if he doesn't click, he'll use Windy again. Windy's through! High as a kite. These Hedgetown fans are tough and they've got the Mules playin' for blood. This isn't baseball, it's murder! You see Willis throwin' those dusters?"

The first hitter Burns faced was Sandy Adams, a block of granite who played third base for the Mules and hit second in the batting order. Burns kept them high, anticipating the bunt, but he had to come in there when the count reached three and one, and Adams pushed a perfect roller down the third-base line. Hale swooped in on the ball like a hawk, fielding it flawlessly, saw the runners were too far along for a successful force, and then threw Adams out by twenty feet. But Willis and Bates were in scoring position on third and second and there was only one away.

Nick Marreno, the Mules' first sacker, worked Burns to the three-and-one count and then blasted a hard liner clear to the wall in right center. Willis and Bates scored and Ted Smith took the rebound from the wall. Marreno turned second when the husky Bear right fielder set himself for the throw and the ball beat the Mules' first sacker to third by fifteen feet. Hale took the throw and poised behind the bag for the out. But Marreno came right on, made no attempt to slide. Instead, he charged head on into the little hundred and fifty pounder. Paul catapulted backward as though hit by a truck and lit on the back of his head. The ball flew up in the air and Marreno cast a mirthless laugh at Hale and dashed on home to score.

Eddie Duer reached home plate at the same time, tearing out of the dugout, dashing for the Mule first sacker. Just as Marreno crossed the plate, Duer grasped the burly fellow and nearly jerked the giant's arm off as he spun him around.

In a second they were going at it hammer and tongs while players from the field and the dugout joined in the melee. The umpires and the field police broke it up almost as soon as it started, but the heated argument which followed resulted in Eddie Duer's banishment

from the field. Somehow, Chip found himself right behind Duer, right in the center of things when the scuffle
started, but he was never able to figure out how he got
there.

Gabby Breen got a hero's ovation as he stalked back
to the third-base coaching box and there was a broad
grin of satisfaction on his face. Marreno's reception by
the fans was less than enthusiastic, even the Hedgetown
fans finding little excuse for his deliberate charge into
the little third sacker. Duer took his time about depart-
ing and the crowd booed him every second he was in
sight.

Bob Reiter took charge of the Bears and spent a long
afternoon juggling pitchers, fielders, hitters, and trying
vainly to stem the hitting assault of the Mules. But at
last the game was over and the Hedgetown fans howled
enthusiastically for their "new deal" and "fighting manager," and promised all and sundry and particularly the
Bear players that they'd be right back on hand the next
afternoon to see a repeat performance. And, as they
slowly left the scene of the massacre, they howled and
jeered the Bears and pointed to the 16–3 score posted
on the board in center field.

The Mule players continued their celebration in the
dressing room, cheering Red Willis and Nick Marreno.
Breen was all over the place, patting the players on
the back, playing up to them and assuring them they'd
give the Bears the same treatment the next afternoon.

"Just keep your eyes on me out in that third-base
coaching box when you're up there with the stick—
that's all you gotta do!"

The Mules had responded to Breen, all right. Not
that he was the kind of man they might have chosen for
a manager, but because he had brought them luck
against their bitter rivals. Most of the Mule players had

been surprised at the choice of Breen. A few had been disappointed, but they all hoped that the change might mean a letup of the bad luck which seemed to have dogged them all year. Tonight, however, flush from the victory and the heart-warming support of the fans for the first time in weeks, they had no thoughts other than this game might be the changing point, the hurdle which might mean the pennant.

Hoot Kearns was nearly as exuberant as his players. The near-record turnout and the play of the Mules had lifted his spirits and he dismissed some of the worries his managing problem had occasioned. That accounted for the big smile he gave Breen when that worthy joined him in the office.

"Nice start, Gabby," Kearns said approvingly.

"Thanks, boss. I told you we'd win, didn't I?"

"You sure did! By the way, Gabby, I thought Willis was throwing a little too close to the hitters and I didn't like the rhubarb Marreno stirred up when he charged into Hale."

"You're right on both counts, boss," Breen agreed. "I spoke to both of them about it."

"They're both a little hard to handle, especially Willis. Don't let them get out of hand."

"Don't worry, boss. I'll run the club."

"I hope so. You've made a good start. Keep it up!"

"Boss—er—you don't mind a little aggressiveness, do you? A winner's gotta be a fighter, you know."

"Well, the right sort of aggressiveness is all right, but I don't go for fighting between players. Let's win playing baseball and leave the fighting for the Friday night boxing shows. Okay?"

Breen was smirking with satisfaction as he made his way to his car. All he needed to pull the wool over Kearns' eyes was a little soft soap. Of course you had to "yes" a big shot like Kearns but that was easy enough. This had sure been a day. Everything had clicked. Now if he could only win tomorrow. Duer probably would start Kildane and the big flagpole was tough. "The Squill treatment oughta take care of Kildane's fast stuff," he muttered happily. "Now for a big steak and then I'll light out for the Circus and wait for Corky."

The Bears were a sad, disgusted crew that night. Gone was the usual dining-room banter and laughter. Chip felt as bad as the rest. He hadn't liked the kind of baseball he had seen today and tried to think of some- thing else. But Corky Squill was in his mind and he went back to the question that had disturbed him all afternoon. Why had Corky Squill changed from a sul- len, morose individualist to a peppy holler guy?

At a near-by table, Boiler Burns, Windy Mills, and Mickey Curry were talking and, without really intend- ing to, Chip listened. Their words registered as clearly as the peal of a bell.

"They sure teed off on me!" Mills said worriedly. "Seemed to know every time I was gonna use my fast ball. I don't get it! They never dug in on me before."

"I don't have much of a fast ball," Burns said lamely, "but every time I tried one, they knocked it out of the park."

"We gotta take those guys tomorrow," Curry growled. "Some club! Manager bench jockeying, pitcher bean balling, base runners playin' football— Huh! Marreno's going to run into something he won't like the next time he scores on *me!*"

Kildane swung around in his chair. "You can expect that kind of baseball from the Mules from now on," he said bitterly. "The manager sets the pace, you know."

On the way out of the dining room Kildane stopped at Hale's table and placed his hands on the little third sacker's shoulders. "Feeling all right, Pauly?" he asked.

Hale nodded. "Neck's a little stiff, but otherwise I'm okay. Never figured he was going to charge me deliberately. Won't happen again!"

"You can say that again," Kildane said grimly.

There was no movie for Chip and Kildane that night. They took their usual after-dinner jaunt and then headed back to the hotel.

"I want to get a good night's rest, Chip. See you in the morning. Night!"

Chip knew what the tall chucker had in mind, all right. Scissors was burning and he was hoping Eddie Duer would let him work the next day's game. Chip hoped so, too, for several reasons. He had studied Scissors Kildane's motions and pitches until he knew them by heart. Tomorrow's game would be a good time to check on something which had been running through his mind all evening. He'd write his mother and the Sugar Bowl crowd a letter and hit the hay, too.

Most of the Bear players had gone to the movies but a few lounged around the lobby reading and talking. No dissipation for this outfit! The Bears played for keeps on and off the field. Eddie Duer was a gentle taskmaster, providing his training and playing rules were observed. But woe to the transgressor! Duer was a tyrant where food and sleep were concerned. He believed a ballplayer was just as good as his food and rest. That was the reason the Bears had the most liberal food allowance in the league and also the reason the twelve-o'clock curfew was inviolate.

Corky Squill was missing from the lobby. But he would have been pleased by the conversation of the Bear players gathered there. In fact, Corky's play on the field that afternoon had been about the only Bear performance worth remembering.

"What hit Corky?" someone asked.

"Got me," Bucky Boyd said quizzically. "I've played next to him nearly two years now, and I never heard him open his mouth before."

"He sure was a holler guy this afternoon," Hale said, shaking his head. "You think Willis made him sore?"

"Could be," Stretch Johnson said thoughtfully.

"Corky would be the best second sacker around," Curry said appraisingly, "if he hustled *every* day like he did this afternoon. I never could figure out why he always clammed up when everyone else was pepping it up."

"Yeah, that's right," Boyd added. "I remember the time Eddie hauled him over the coals, tried to get him to do a little talkin', and Corky just stood there as if he was dumb, never said a word. Eddie finally got disgusted and left him alone."

"He's hard to crack," Johnson said wryly. "I guess I know Corky Squill better than anyone on the club but that still leaves him and me strangers. I wish I could figure him out."

At that moment Corky Squill was at the Circus Drive-In Court talking with Gabby Breen. Perhaps listening would be more accurate, for Squill hardly had a chance to get a word in edgewise. Breen was wound up, excited, exuberant, and, as usual, careless with the truth.

"Kearns was so happy he promised me a bonus. Imagine that! The first day! I told you he was that kind of a guy! Wait till you get on his pay roll, you'll find out. What a start! And you know what! He told me right after the game the Bears would be just an ordinary ball club without you and Mickey Curry. Of course he mentioned Kildane. How's that?"

Squill nodded and started to speak but the first word

was barely formed on his tongue when Breen was off again.

"He's comin' our way, Corky—fast! All you gotta do is keep up the good work. You looked great out there today. You can clinch him tomorrow. Why, about all he talked about besides the win was your playin'."

While Breen talked, he watched Squill closely. He had noticed the surly second baseman's coolness at the initial greeting and was utilizing all his persuasive talking powers to disarm Squill before giving him a chance to talk. Eventually, however, Breen talked himself into a spot which gave Squill an opening.

"How didya like Willis today?" Breen demanded proudly. "Had his stuff, didn't he?"

"Yeah, he had his stuff, all right," Squill retorted. "I shoulda parted his hair with a bat in the third when he threw his fast ball at my head. That bean ball stuff your idea or his?"

"Not mine, Corky," Breen quickly assured the irate player. "Me, I don't go for that kind of chuckin' unless the hitters ask for it, crowd the plate. Eddie musta been boilin'!"

Squill nodded. "He sure was! In fact, the whole club's boilin'. I don't feel too good about you guys myself and you might as well know it now as any other time. I ain't goin' to take no bean ball stuff from anyone and that goes double for Willis."

Breen was thoroughly alarmed. He couldn't afford to have Corky kicking over the traces now. So he turned on all his charm and went to work. And when Squill left just in time to beat Eddie Duer's curfew, Breen and his former protégé were again on friendly terms.

CHAPTER 12

DUGOUT JINX

CHIP HILTON was a normal youngster in every way. He had ambitions beyond his college days, of course, but along with those he wanted to excel as an athlete. Chip was smart enough to know that, other things being equal, the best competitor was the fellow who was well conditioned, able to give his best performance all the time. That was why Chip was careful to eat regularly and get plenty of rest. Usually his day was so full of action that he had no trouble falling asleep as soon as his head hit the pillow. But that had not been the case during the past week. The travel, change of scenes, new faces, and the excitement which accompanies a team on the road had disrupted his normal way of life. Then there was Corky Squill. The Bears' pivot star was the center of Chip's thoughts every night and tonight was no exception.

Chip tossed and turned, trying to figure out the cause of Squill's sudden change of attitude. Corky had been exceedingly friendly until the day of the race. Chip thought back, trying to figure why the mere loss of a foot race would cause such a change. It didn't make sense. Then he remembered that Squill's attitude had changed even before the race. It had been obvious that something was wrong when Corky didn't answer him when he spoke to him on the way to the outfield to shag flies. Corky must have heard him, for he wasn't more than ten feet away. Chip had said, "I'm backing you up, Corky. Don't worry about a thing," and Squill had deliberately turned his back. So something must have happened even before that.

Chip's thoughts unaccountably shifted to Gabby Breen, and he began to wonder if Squill's animosity was due to his refusal to sign Breen's contract. That didn't make much sense either, except that the two men were friends. This thought started Chip off on another tangent and it was hours before he finally succeeded in getting to sleep.

Most of the Bear players slept late the day of a game and ate a combined breakfast-lunch before going out for hitting and fielding practice. Chip got up early but he always waited for Kildane to come down to the lobby so he could have brunch with his pitcher friend. That was why he had time to read the story of the previous afternoon's game in the Sunday *Courier*. As he expected, the Mules got a great write-up.

Mules Overwhelm Bears 16–3

WILLIS TRIUMPHS OVER BEAR PITCHING STAFF

Nick Marreno's grand slam homer and the near-perfect pitching of lefty Red Willis were high lights of the Mules' surprise walloping of the league-leading Bears yesterday afternoon. The victory was a nice welcome for the Mules' new manager, George "Gabby" Breen, and gave the local fans new pennant hopes. The win cuts the Bears' games won lead to four with three less defeats in the loss column.

Willis was dazzling, limiting the visitors to four scattered hits while his teammates were amassing twenty-one safe bingles, nine for extra bases. Eddie Duer, banished in the bottom of the second, started Windy Mills, shifted him to left field while Boiler Burns gave it a try, brought in Akers for two-thirds of an inning, got Richards to last for two, and finally ended up with his starting pitcher, Mills.

Marreno stepped to the plate with two aboard in the bottom of the second, and, on the three-and-one pitch, walloped Boiler Burns' toss against the right center wall to score Willis and Bates. Marreno scored on the play when Hale dropped the ball in a collision at third.

Breen is expected to start Skids Baker this afternoon, but Eddie Duer was undecided early this morning about his choice. A win this afternoon might give the Mules the momentum they need to make the race a dingdong affair. After today, the Mules have ten more games to play, six with the Bears. It is conceivable that the championship will be decided in the final two-game series which will be played here September 3 and 4.

"Doesn't read too good, does it?"

Chip glanced up in surprise. He hadn't heard Duer and Kildane approach, but when he saw who it was, he rose quickly to his feet. "It sure doesn't," he said, smiling wryly.

"Throw that away and read tomorrow's story," Kildane said grimly.

Chip shot a questioning glance at the Bear manager. Duer nodded his head.

"Yep," he said lamely, "wouldn't let me come down for breakfast until I said he could pitch today. Come on. Let's get some eats."

While they breakfasted, Duer reviewed the Mules' batting order for Kildane.

"You know Bates—bats righty, crowds the plate, waits 'em out, hits a fast ball straight away. Doesn't like 'em around his wrists.

"Adams hits lefty, likes soft stuff, will pull everything except your screwball and an outside pitch.

"Marreno hits lefty, likes 'em around the letters, can't handle anything you throw around the knees.

"Fellows bats from the third-base side of the plate, takes a big cut. Mix 'em up, keep him off balance.

"Conover hits right, likes to dig in, takes a long stride. Can't handle the hooks.

"Roth bats right, pulls 'em, and is a sucker for the high inside pitch.

"Kinkaid is a cutie, crowds the right side of the plate, likes to wait 'em out. Can't hit the fast ball.

"Berry will watch everything below his waist go by, especially fast stuff. He's a sucker for a sinker or anything resembling a screwball.

"Baker couldn't hit a soft ball!

"Well, that's it, Scissors. I guess you know 'em as well as I do. Wish you'd skip this game, though. Take a rest. There's lots of time left and we've got seven more with the Mules."

But Kildane would have none of that. Duer had said "yes" and Scissors meant to hold the manager to his word. On the way to the park in the bus, Kildane sat with Chip and again went through the Mules' batting order.

"Eddie always runs through the other club's batting order before a game," Kildane explained. "I guess you've heard him before. We do the same thing out in the bull pen while we're watching the game. That's usually Duster Reed's job. He's in charge of the bull pen, but he's sick, in the hospital. Guess you didn't meet him. Might be back for the last game or so—"

The arrival at the ball park cut short further conversation and the Bears dressed hurriedly, anxious to get out on the field and get at the Mules. Maybe it was this very eagerness which tightened them up or maybe they tried too hard. At any rate, the umpire's "Play ball" did not lead to the ring of Bear bats against the ball. In fact, Squill, Boyd, and Dawson went down in order, much in the same fashion of the previous afternoon. And when Scissors Kildane toed the rubber and faced the first Mule hitter, Butch Bates, he got the same treatment the crowd had accorded Windy Mills.

The crowd roar was one continuous jumble of sound. "Here you go, Kildane!" "Off to the races!" "Murder the bums!"

Chip had watched the ball fly around the infield, from Curry to Squill to Johnson to Hale to Boyd and back to Johnson, and he felt a premonition, felt the strain the Bears had evidenced in the clubhouse. Nerves had been stretched to the breaking point and it was apparent by the sharpness in their voices and the shortness of their tempers. It had struck Chip while he was dressing and he had tried to keep in the background, keep quiet, remain as unobtrusive as possible. No one had seemed to notice him except Corky Squill who had waited until Duer had left for the field to follow and utter one word—"jinx"—out of the side of his mouth as he passed.

Chip sat in the corner of the dugout now, watching Scissors go into his windup. The slender chucker had seemed right in his warm-up, had fired the ball across the plate like a flash of light. Chip watched the lead-off hitter, Butch Bates. Bates looked at Gabby Breen in the third-base coaching box and Chip followed the glance, knew some sort of a sign had passed between the two, but hadn't been able to catch it. Before he could turn his head back to the plate he heard the crack of bat on ball and saw the sphere flying directly over second base; a perfect Texas leaguer. Bates had singled on the first ball pitched.

The Mule fans were in a frenzy. They had risen to their feet as one man. They were cheering Bates to the skies, while a crescendo of advice and sundry remarks flooded out toward Kildane. But the bingle hadn't upset Kildane. He stood just back of the mound, the resin bag in his fingers, looking down the alley at Mickey Curry. Then he stepped to the rubber and took his stretch. Chip had again caught the hitter, Adams who hit lefty, watching Breen in the third-base coaching box. He figured the play was a sacrifice. So did Kildane, for the ball came in fast and hard and across the shoulders on the outside for a called strike. Scissors wasted two and then evened the count with a hook which jug-handled right across the middle. So it was two and two.

Adams stepped out of the batter's box then and glanced down the third-base line at Breen. But Breen was looking out toward the outfield and Adams reluctantly stepped back up to the plate. Then Curry gave Kildane the sign and Scissors toed the rubber. Chip was watching Adams like a hawk and caught the look he gave Breen, but he was too late to catch the sign, if sign there was. However, he saw Adams step into the pitch, high outside, and send the ball scampering behind the runner between Squill and Johnson. Stretch made a try but was a step too far away. Chip groaned, then leaped to his feet with a cry of joy. Corky Squill had darted far to his left, scooped up the ball with his glove hand, pivoted, and threw to Boyd scampering across the key-stone bag to catch Bates by a step. Then Bucky made one of these impossible throws, clawing the air with his feet and throwing from his precarious position above the sliding Bates. But the ball beat Adams by a whisper and the umpire jerked his thumb over his shoulder. It was as pretty a double play as you would ever want to see. Even the Hedgetown fans responded with a scattering of handclaps.

Chip breathed easier. That was more like it! But he knew that Bates and Adams had both hit the ball solidly, too solidly for comfort. Nick Marreno stalked up to the plate, scowling and pounding his bat on the ground. The crowd cheered and Chip shot a quick glance at Kildane. He could tell by the expression on the tall chucker's face that he was out to get the burly first sacker. Chip remembered Duer's warning: "Marreno likes 'em around the letters, can't handle anything you throw around the knees."

Marreno glanced at Breen in the coaching box and then stepped to the plate. Kildane whipped a fast ball smack across the middle of the platter for strike one. The ball had been right at the knees. The next pitch was an angled hook which swooped across the inside corner for called strike number two.

"Atta boy, Scissors, strike the big mug out! Can't hit 'em if he can't see them!" Squill's blast carried clear into the dugout and Chip eyed the second sacker in astonishment. Corky was in front of second base waving his arms and jumping up and down as though he were crazy, and he was still there when Kildane fogged his fast one low outside for ball one.

"Right in there!" Squill boomed. "Put on your glasses, Robber!"

The umpire's response was to call "time" and stalk out to the side of the plate and call Eddie Duer. Chip couldn't hear what was being said, but Duer went out behind the mound and talked to Squill, and Corky waved a contemptuous hand at the umpire and moved back to his normal position.

"Claims Corky's obstructing the vision of the hitter,"

Duer said briefly, as he dropped down into the dugout.

"Move him out of there, Scissors," Squill yelled. "Give him a little of his own medicine."

Marreno stepped out of the box and glared angrily at Squill. But if he expected to squelch Corky with that weapon, he was disappointed. Squill placed the thumbs of his meat hand and his glove beside his ears and wiggled his fingers. The gesture infuriated Marreno, and Kildane's knee-high slider set the burly first baseman down on a called third strike.

Marreno whirled on the plate umpire's "s-t-e-e-r-i-k-e" and it seemed for a second as if he meant to attack the arbiter. Shouting at the top of his voice he shook the bat menacingly at the impassive man in blue and protested the decision.

Corky Squill came trotting in then, again wiggling his fingers at his ears and Marreno nearly exploded. But Squill kept going, laughing at the infuriated man, and the interruption served to distract Marreno's attention from the umpire. Relieved from the tension, the Bears came hustling into the dugout yelling and determined to "go get some runs!"

Skids Baker was a righty, fast, and equipped with a darting slider and a sharp hook. When he was right, he was tough. And he was right today. Squill topped one of the swooping curves and it dribbled down the third-base line. Bates threw him out easily. Boyd struck out and Dawson lifted a high fly to right field. So it was three up and three down before Kildane hardly had time to snuggle into his jacket and wipe his brow.

The Mules continued their sharp hitting in the second, third, and fourth. But, luckily, as in the opening frame, a Bear infielder or outfielder was in the right spot. Kildane said nothing, but Chip could tell he was worried by the consistent ring of the Mule bats. Skids

Baker, on the other hand, was having one of his big days. The husky right-hander was fast and right, and the Bears' wood work had been limited to one safe bingle, a screaming liner in the fourth by Corky Squill which was good for three. But Squill had died there; his teammates hadn't gotten the ball past the infield.

In the bottom of the fifth, Kildane's luck deserted him. Bingo Berry, the Mule receiver, led off with a clean single, meeting one of Kildane's fast balls right on the nose. Chip caught the look of astonishment on Kildane's face and the warning glance Mickey Curry flashed toward Eddie Duer in the dugout. Then Skids Baker crossed up everyone in the park. Kildane played him for the advance but the big chucker met the high, fast ball flush on the nose, pushing a looping liner to short right field.

Kildane really tried on Butch Bates. But the stocky shortstop, hitting from the first-base side of the plate, connected with a fast ball, sending it inside the right-field foul line all the way to the fence. It was a perfect hit with runners on first and second, behind them, and good for a double, even though Ted Smith had played the pull hitter correctly. Berry and Bates scored and the Hedgetown fans nearly tore down the stands. It didn't stop there. Sandy Adams walked and Nick Marreno evened his score with Kildane by golfing one of Scissors' fast balls into right field for a clean single, scoring Bates and sending Adams to third. Jack Fellows followed and blasted a hard ground ball along the third-base line, which Hale miraculously knocked down. Adams started home but scurried back when Hale recovered the ball. So the bases were loaded with none away and Duer called "time" and hurried out to the mound.

Chip could see Kildane shaking his head while Duer

talked and he knew his pitcher friend didn't want to be relieved. The Hedgetown fans added fuel to Kildane's fire of determination by booing and catcalling. This was the first time in two years that the Mules had been able to shake the confidence of the Bears' pitching star and the crowd ate it up. And they gave Eddie Duer a good going over when he made his way back to the dugout. Bob Reiter cast an inquisitive glance at the worried manager.

"Says he's right," Duer said briefly.

"What did Mickey say?"

"Same thing! Can't understand it! Says Scissors is workin' beautifully. Puttin' 'em right where they oughta go—unless the hitting dope we have on these guys is all wet."

Chip concentrated on the next hitter, Pete Conover. Duer had said the Mules' right fielder was a power hitter, took a long stride, and couldn't hit a curve. Conover disproved that statement on the first pitch. Kildane came in with his darting hook which dipped toward the bottom of the strike zone. Perhaps it would be more accurate to say it started to dip, because Conover stepped into the curve and his bat met the ball right on the nose. There was a tense second of stillness while every person in the park followed the flight of the ball. Then a great roar burst over the field as the ball cleared the left field fence and disappeared. It was a home run!

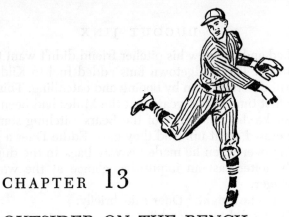

CHAPTER **13**

OUTSIDER ON THE BENCH

SCISSORS KILDANE had been a pitching sensation ever since he joined the Bears. The big fellow had known one success after another. True, he had suffered a few defeats but the contests had been close, anybody's game right up to the bottom of the ninth. But he had never been humiliated, had never known the bitter frustration which grips a chucker who has all his stuff, good control, feels right, yet is unable to get his offerings past the hitters.

Chip suffered with Kildane through the rest of that disastrous game, threw every pitch, and felt the same disheartening pangs when the Mule hitters teed off and drove in run after run. And he was swinging with every Bear hitter as they tried desperately to get some runs. But it was no use and Chip was as glad as the Bears to hurry into the clubhouse after their last time at bat in the ninth. But he did cast one despairing glance at the scoreboard to note the seventeen hits and fourteen runs in the Mules' column. Chip didn't need to read the Bear totals. He knew them by heart.

Behind him, in the stands and in the bleachers, the Hedgetown fans were celebrating. And, in the home team clubhouse, the Mules were jubilantly talking, shouting, and laughing.

"We poured it on them," Breen proclaimed loudly. "But good!"

"Guess we gave Kildane his lumps," someone shouted.

"About time," another added.

"We've got 'em now," Breen declared. "We'll murder the Bears every time! Wait and see! All you guys gotta do is watch me when you're up at that dish."

Tim Murphy, the Mules' head coach, shook his head admiringly.

"You sure called 'em today!" he chuckled. "I don't know how you're doin' it, but you're sure hittin' 'em right on the nose!"

"Leave that to me," Breen said, basking appreciatively in Murphy's praise. Then he sobered. "All right, now. No game tomorrow, so no curfew tonight. But everyone on hand tomorrow at four o'clock at the depot. Nice goin' today! Let's take two from the Leopards!"

Over under the third-base stands the Bears dressed in silence, the heavy silence indicative of their mood. And, although nothing was said, there wasn't a person in the room who didn't feel sorry for Scissors Kildane. Kildane had shown he could take it, had kept bearing down all the way, stuck it out in the face of the terrific razzing the Hedgetown fans had directed his way all afternoon and had asked Duer to let him face it out. Kildane was no quitter and he wasn't looking for sympathy.

Eddie Duer was last off the field. He came hustling into the room showing none of the tension the four straight losses had built up in his heart. And his words, spoken in soft, even tones were reassuring and confident.

"Don't worry about it! We were bad—so what! We're out in front and we're going to stay there. We're home for two in a row starting Tuesday and—by the way— we'll work out tomorrow at three o'clock. Now get a move on. We've got forty minutes to catch the train. Sooner we're out of this burg the better! We can chow up in the diner!"

Chip always got a thrill out of eating on a train. Most of the Bears did, too. He followed them forward before the train pulled out of the Hedgetown depot. Chip sat beside Kildane; Eddie Duer and Mickey Curry sat on the opposite side of the table. Nothing much was said until they reached dessert. Then Curry voiced everyone's thoughts, abruptly speaking out as if he was resuming an earlier conversation.

"Seemed to be ready for every pitch! Dug in for fast stuff, stepped into curves, watched the bad ones go by. I don't get it!"

"Just as if they knew what was comin'," Kildane added.

"Could be, you know," Duer said thoughtfully. "It's been done before."

"You mean the signs?" Curry asked.

Duer nodded. "Yes and no! Could be Gabby Breen's stealin' the signs and it could be he's stealin' them from you."

"Me?" Curry demanded.

"Yes, you or Scissors. Could be you hold your mitt in one position for fast balls and in another position for curves. And it could be Scissors if he's using a different windup for different pitches."

"Gee, I've been careful about that ever since I've been with you, Eddie," Kildane said earnestly. "Why, I think about that every time I throw. Chip and I were talking about it a couple of days ago."

"I know, Scissors," Duer said kindly. "Don't worry about it. I was doping out the possibilities. Personally, I don't think Gabby Breen's that smart. Another thing, keep in mind this could have been one of those days.

"Every team has days once in a while when even the umpires can't get 'em out. We've had 'em and there's no reason the Mules can't have 'em! Anyway, it's water over the dam. See you in the morning. They're settin' our car off in Parkville, so you can sleep as long as you like."

Most of the Bears sat in the club car until it was time to go to bed, and Chip and Scissors joined them. At first there was a feeling of tension and little conversation. But a club car does something to any group and the Bears were soon chatting easily, the defeats apparently forgotten.

Chip left around ten o'clock and clambered into his upper berth. Usually the rushing sound of the train and the clickety-clack of the wheels carried him into a quick slumber. But his thoughts wouldn't be stilled, couldn't be coaxed or tricked away from the Mules and the defeats and, strangely enough, from Gabby Breen. And Kildane's words kept running through his mind. "You know, Chip, they seemed to be ready for anything I served 'em. I don't get it! Smokes, they never dug in on me before. Why, they planted themselves up there just as if they were getting the signs."

"Just as if they were getting the signs!" The phrase came back again and again until the repetitive monotony eventually lulled him into a troubled sleep.

Three o'clock the following afternoon found Chip chasing flies in Bear Stadium. Eddie Duer believed in practice, lots of practice. And the Bear players worked hard, putting out in practice just as they put out in the games. These kids were hustlers. Eddie Duer needled

them just a bit before hitting practice. Not too much,
because the wily little manager realized the importance
of easing up on a beaten team and pouring it on a
cocky, winning team.

"Maybe we oughta sharpen up our battin' eyes a
little," he said dryly. "Chip, s'pose you serve 'em up.
We'll hit in our regular batting order for five or six
rounds. Mickey, you do the receivin'. Hit three and lay
one down. Then I wanta see some speed when you circle the bases. Let's go!"

Chip was already loose and needed only a few
warm-up pitches before Corky Squill tapped the plate
with his bat. Squill sent a cautious glance over his
shoulder to make sure Eddie Duer was out of hearing
and then drawled insolently, "Throw me that jinx ball,
Hilton. I wanta knock it down your throat!"

Chip's face flushed scarlet, but he said nothing. Instead, he turned and dusted his fingers with the resin
bag while he regained control of his emotions.

"All right, Rabbit Ears," Squill muttered again,
"throw me that nothin' ball of yours!'"

Mickey Curry thumped his big fist into the catcher's
mitt. "Lay off, Corky," he growled good-naturedly. "Let
the kid alone."

Squill whirled about, his eyes flashing angrily as he
glared at the big receiver. "Keep your trap out of this,"
he snarled.

"Take it easy, Corky," Curry said quickly. "You'll
make the kid mad and he'll strike you out."

"Strike me out," Squill ridiculed. "Huh! That'll be
the day!"

The doughty second sacker stepped out of the batter's box and then glanced toward the dugout where
Eddie Duer was talking to Bob Reiter. Then he glared

angrily in Chip's direction. "Come on, Bad News," he growled. "Let's see you strike me out!"

But Chip ignored Squill and served up a straight hard one which split the plate.

"Right in there, Corky," Curry said softly. "What's the matter? Too fast?"

"You mean that was a fast ball?" Squill retorted, laughing harshly. "Huh, that pitch wouldn't break a pane of glass."

Curry grunted and carried the ball out to the mound. "Strike him out, Chip," he said earnestly. "Show the little troublemaker up!"

But Chip wasn't interested in striking out Corky Squill or anyone else right then. Eddie Duer wanted his ballplayers to get hitting practice and had told Chip to lay the ball across the plate. So Chip smiled and shook his head.

"Guess I'd better just throw 'em over straight, Mickey," he said.

"Okay, Chip," Curry said resignedly, "but it wouldn't make anyone mad. Corky's askin' for it an' he oughta get it."

So Squill banged three lusty drives into left center and then dropped a pretty bunt down the first-base line. And, as he dug toward first, he sent the bat slithering along the ground nearly to the mound, leaving no doubt in any observer's mind that he was out to get the kid chucker. With the exception of Scissors Kildane and Mickey Curry, the Bear players weren't taking sides in the argument. But there was concern in their eyes when they glanced at one another. Next to Scissors, Corky Squill was the most important player in the Bear line-up and a feud between their star chucker and the keystone sacker could mean a lot of trouble in their drive for the pennant. There was no further argument during the rest of the afternoon but it broke out anew that night in the hotel lobby. This time it was an open break between Kildane and the morose infielder. Squill was complaining bitterly to Stretch Johnson when the tall chucker sauntered out of the dining room with Chip.

"Outsiders don't belong on the bench," Squill said pointedly, swinging around to look full into Kildane's face.

"You talking to me?" Kildane asked coolly.

"I'm tellin' you," Squill said angrily. "Outsiders don't belong in the dugout even if they *are* stooges for the big shot of the club."

"I don't know any stooges and I don't know any big shots, Corky," Kildane drawled, "but I do know you're acting like a spoiled brat."

Squill's face flushed darkly. "Maybe you'd like to try a little correctin'," he snarled.

"Maybe I would, and maybe I will," Kildane drawled.

"What's the matter with right now?" Squill demanded. But he was talking to Kildane's back. The chucker had turned away and had headed for Chip, who was waiting near the door. Without a word the two friends made their way up the street toward their favorite movie theater. Their silence was more expressive than words. Both were embarrassed and conversation was difficult.

Chip didn't enjoy the picture that night. In fact, he couldn't have told you much about it because he was trying to figure out the cause of Corky Squill's sudden animosity. He was still trying to figure it out the next afternoon while the Bears were lacing the Bluebirds 13 to 2. And all through the game he watched Corky Squill and tried to puzzle out the reason for the difficulty. Chip knew something had happened to change Squill's attitude. Not only with respect to their personal relations but with Squill's actions on the field. Right then, the chunky second sacker was pepping it up, seemingly at ease with the world.

"Come on, Softy Boy. We're back of you, kid. Attaboy!"

The win over the Bluebirds had been a must, for the Mules carved out a neat 6–1 score over the Leopards to keep pace in the stretch race and give Breen his third straight victory as the new Hedgetown manager. Breen was on top of the world and advertised the fact to everyone within hearing distance. And he didn't neglect H. B. Kearns. Right after the end of the ninth, when the last Leopard hitter had been retired, Breen rushed to the telephone. He knew the Mules' owner would be in his office listening in on the game.

"Hello, Mr. Kearns—Gabby! . . . Yes, sir, we had 'em all the way. . . . We're sure gonna try! I'm plannin' on Berg for tomorrow. . . . Right! Turner for the Bears on Saturday. We've gotta win that one!"

Breen's face wore a satisfied look when he finished his conversation with the owner of the Mules. Everything was breaking just right. The Mules were only two and a half games back of the league leaders now, and if they could keep step until Saturday, Lefty Turner might continue his mastery over the Bears with his wild southpaw hooks and dusters.

But the wily manager's luck changed the very next day. The Leopards pounded Berg for fourteen hits and downed the Mules 7 to 3. For the Bears, Eddie Duer gambled on Phil Akers and the relief chucker came through beautifully, whitewashing the Bluebirds while his teammates bunched their hits to score a 6–0 victory. So the Bears chalked up victory 94 against 53 losses while the Mules added another defeat giving them a total of 90 and 56.

There's nothing like a win or two to cheer up a ballplayer. Team victories and a fattening of the batting average serves to erase almost everything. Scissors Kildane was such a loyal team player that he was almost his old self again, too. But he still couldn't forget the pasting by the Mules.

"I can't understand it," Kildane said grimly, as he and Chip relaxed in the lobby of the Park Hotel that evening. "It's the first time the Mules ever hit me consistently."

"You think Mr. Duer might be right about Gabby Breen getting the signs?"

Kildane shook his head decisively. "No, I don't! Curry's like a wooden Indian behind the plate. No, it's not Mickey and I don't think it's me. Why, I practiced before a mirror for two years so I'd use the same motion for every pitch—still do!"

Chip carried the problem to bed and into his dreams that night but could find no answer. Every tangent ended in a blind alley. And every time his thoughts came to a blank wall, Corky Squill appeared on the scene waving a tremendous bat and grinning diabolically as he challenged Chip to "strike me out!"

The Bears were idle the next two days, but Eddie Duer had them out at Bear Stadium each morning. Thursday passed without incident because Chip was careful to give Squill plenty of room. But the ill feeling between Kildane and Squill came to a head during the Friday morning workout and Eddie Duer was caught right in the middle of the trouble. Chip was throwing for batting practice and Squill was baiting him every time Duer was out of hearing. Mickey Curry and Scissors Kildane retaliated by needling the second sacker whenever his turn come to bat.

"Can't hit the size of his hat, Chip," Curry chortled. "Feed him a fast ball and watch him duck!"

"Breaks his back on a hook," Kildane added.

"Ain't no swell-headed kid gonna strike me out," Squill retorted. "Come on, Jinx, throw me one of your high school balls!"

From all appearances, Eddie Duer had been completely oblivious to the brewing feud between Squill and Kildane. But a keen observer would have known better, would have known that Duer's success as a baseball coach wasn't due entirely to his knowledge of the game. In fact, Duer's leadership, personality, and extensive use of psychology was his chief strength. He had seen this trouble coming and decided it would be best to bring the matter to a head. So he maneuvered about the field until the stage was set and then appeared on the scene just in time to hear Squill's remark. He was worried but one couldn't tell it. His bearing suggested only that he considered the whole thing a bit of horseplay. But he noticed the tension which centered around the belligerent infielder as he moved into action.

"Go ahead, Chip," he called, "go ahead. I'm neutral so I'll call 'em."

Duer walked briskly out behind the mound and the ribbing ceased. Chip was nervous because of the awkwardness of his position and his heart wasn't in the chore. But he made up his mind to do his best. Mickey Curry called Chip halfway in to the plate and gave him the signs.

"One finger for your fast one, Chip. Two for your hook, three for your change-up—what do you call it, a blooper?"

Chip toed the rubber and blazed his fast ball tight inside for ball one. Then Curry called for a hook which Squill watched swoop in and across to even the count. Chip came back with his slider, which side-winged like a flash of lightning across the letters and he was ahead, one and two. Another hook swept in and Squill got a piece of it, fouling it back to the screen. Then Chip blazed in a crossfire fast ball which just missed the plate. His slider sizzled in again just missing the inside corner and driving Squill back from the plate to make it the full count.

Squill was white with anger but he didn't lose his head, didn't let it get the best of him. Instead, he was deadly serious, concentrating intently upon Chip and the last big throw. Looking at the players and noting the intentness of each, one would have thought this was the final pitch of a tight World Series championship game.

Chip shook Curry off until Mickey called for the change-up. He knew Squill was right for that kind of pitch after the fast ball and the slider, and his windup was fast and complete. But the ball looped high in the air, catching Squill off balance. Halfway through his swing, Squill checked the bat, tried to slow down to meet the high, looping pitch Chip called his blooper. But Squill had gone too far, could only lunge at the lazy floater which dropped past his bat and into Curry's big glove for strike three.

Scissors Kildane broke the silence. "Nice throwin', Chipper. That one broke his back. What's the matter, Corky? I thought no high school chucker could strike you out?"

Squill whirled about and glared at Kildane for a split second. Then he hurled his bat straight at the tall pitcher. Kildane leaped sideways and twisted away, but the spinning bat thudded into his left side. The blow nearly knocked Kildane down but he kept his feet, clutching his ribs and bending nearly double with the pain. There was a shocked silence broken by Duer's angry denunciation of Squill before he joined the throng of players who surrounded the injured chucker.

"What's the matter with you, Corky? You crazy?" Duer shouted. "Now you get into the clubhouse and out of that uniform. You're suspended as of now. And that little display of temper will cost you five hundred dollars! And I mean to make it stick!"

Eddie Duer figured five hundred dollars and suspension was a stiff penalty. But he didn't know, then, that Scissors Kildane had suffered two cracked ribs and would be out of the game for a week, maybe the rest of the season.

CHAPTER 14

GRANDSTAND TROUBLE SHOOTER

Corky Squill sat in the reception room outside William Malloy's private office. As he sat there, perspiring and fretting, Squill could hear the mumble of voices and he knew his baseball future was hanging in the balance. The news of Scissors Kildane's cracked ribs had spread through pennant-mad Parkville like wildfire. The rumors had spread, too, but the real story was the property of the Bear players, the coaching staff, and Chip Hilton. That was due to Eddie Duer's explicit instructions that all details were to be released only through the club's publicity staff.

Yes, Corky Squill was perspiring and fretting and trying to build up a case in his own mind against Scissors Kildane. But he was finding it difficult to justify any position that would place the blame for his predicament on the popular chucker. Indeed, if he could have heard Kildane right then, Corky Squill would have been extremely confused. Because, at that very moment, Scissors Kildane was pleading the cause of Squill with Eddie Duer and the club owner, William Malloy.

"Look, Mr. Malloy," Kildane said earnestly, "it wasn't

all Corky's fault. We'd been riding him and I guess I poured it on heavier than anybody, and the way the Mules are going, we're going to need every man, every game."

That Eddie Duer didn't go along with Scissors' plea was apparent from his set jaw and the determined light in his eyes. "I don't agree, Scissors," he said firmly. "Corky has been looking for trouble for the past two weeks—" He waved Kildane into silence as he continued.

"Just a minute, now. I know exactly how you feel and I appreciate your team spirit but this is a disciplinary matter. Corky's got to grow up."

Kildane nodded soberly. "You're right, there, Eddie, but I'm speaking for the team and I know how they feel. We had a meeting and they appointed me chairman. The whole bunch of us want to forget it, carry on as if it hadn't happened."

Bill Malloy smiled. "I think I understand, Scissors," he said gently. "S'pose you just leave it to Eddie and me and let us work it out. Okay?"

William Malloy knew exactly what had happened at the team meeting. So did Eddie Duer. They both knew Kildane had called the meeting, had assumed the blame for the trouble, and had influenced his teammates to intercede in Squill's behalf. So, for several minutes after Kildane's departure, they sat quietly considering the problem. Duer broke the silence.

"What do you think, Mr. Malloy?"

What Bill Malloy thought took a long time to express. But two hours later Corky Squill knew the five-hundred-dollar fine was to stick and he knew he had been reinstated only because Scissors Kildane had interceded in his behalf. But Corky Squill wasn't clever enough nor big enough to figure out the "why" of the

matter. He figured Scissors Kildane was "chicken" or
was trying to protect the money he had at stake in the
championship race. And when he clambered aboard
the train at five o'clock that afternoon the only part of
the affair which worried him was the loss of the five
hundred dollars. At eleven-five that night, right after
the Bears checked into their hotel in Hedgetown, Squill
made a beeline for the nearest phone booth and called
Gabby Breen.

Breen greeted Squill's call gleefully. "Boy, are we
clickin'," he chortled. "Kearns is walkin' on air! . . .
Whaddaya mean lucky? Say, what's the straight dope
on Kildane? Report here is he was hurt in battin' practice. . . . You sound like there's more to it— By the
way, Kearns thinks you're great. Give him a good show
tomorrow, kid! We're in! You looked great here last
week. Kearns says you're a real holler guy! . . . Sure
it's what I want! Now, look! Call me next Tuesday. Be
sure to put all the trimmin's on tomorrow."

Squill was well pleased with Gabby Breen and with
himself as well when he slid out of the telephone booth.
This time next year he'd be with Breen, and the Bears
and Eddie Duer and Scissors Kildane and Chip Hilton
would be nothing but a memory. And if Hoot Kearns
liked hustling holler guys— Wait until tomorrow afternoon!

The Hedgetown fans were running a pennant fever.
Every person in town could have told you that the
league-leading Bears had won 94 and lost 53 for a per-
centage of 6394, while the up-and-coming home team
had won 90 and lost 56 for a 6164 standing. And they
were jamming the gates two hours before game time so
they could work out on the Bear players. And work out
they did, shifting their attention from player to player
but missing no one. Particularly Scissors Kildane.

"Hey! Kildane! What happened? Forget to duck?"

"Mighty convenient, Scissors! Saves you a beating!"

"You're all washed up, anyway, Kildane! The Mules own you now!"

"Bye-bye, Bears! We're chasin' you right out of the race!"

The Mules seemed to have pennant fever, too, for they trampled all over the Bears. In the top half of the fourth, with the Mules leading 7 to 2, Corky Squill started to stomp back and forth in the dugout griping and beefing about the jinx. Then he mixed up the bats, poured water on the handles, and generally put on a show. Chip knew the display was chiefly for him and his blood was boiling as he sat there unable to say or do a thing. But he could and did watch Squill's antics in the field.

"Maybe he does it when he's mad, or nervous, or showing off," Chip murmured to himself. But Chip's better judgment told him that wasn't the answer. Squill was a cool customer and a fine player. He wasn't the kind to freeze up, get the apple. So far as Chip could figure it, Corky Squill was at his best when the going was tough.

Kildane was out in the bull pen, his ribs bandaged. But he was in uniform and he was tossing the ball, grimacing each time. And he remained there while his pitching mates tried vainly to stem the flood of Mule hits. When the last Bear hitter struck out in the top of the ninth, Kildane walked slowly to the dugout and joined Chip.

"Don't understand it, Chip," Kildane said wearily. "We used to own them. I can't dope it out!"

Chip wasn't trying to dope out the Mules' sudden mastery of the Bear pitchers, but he was trying to figure out Corky Squill. Against the Bluebirds, the stocky in-

fielder had gone back into his shell, had played silently
and without waste motion. Today he had been a regular jumping jack, brandishing his arms, kicking dirt
with his spikes, charging up to the pitcher's box, moving
nervously from side to side, and generally behaving
like a whirling dervish. Squill had been solid enough in
his play. In fact, he had been the Bears' shining light,
getting three for four at bat and fielding his position
faultlessly. Not that it mattered much in the score, for
the Mules were the masters, piling up an easy 14–4
victory.

The Hedgetown rooters were in a frenzy. They took
over the ball park, swarming out on the field and under
the stands and right up against the door of the Mules'
clubhouse. Inside, the Mule players roughhoused and
yelled friendly insults at one another while Hoot Kearns
and Gabby Breen sat in the manager's room and cele-
brated the victory.

"Nice win, Gabby," Kearns said happily.

"I told you we'd do it!" Breen boasted. "We own
'em! With or without Scissors Kildane!"

Kearns didn't have a chance to talk much thereafter.
Breen was bubbling over with joy and spouting words
like a linotype machine.

"Five more games with those guys, three at Parkville
and two here. Oh, boy! The way we're goin' and with
Kildane out, we might take it. Heck, if we can knock
'em off two of the three in Parkville, we're a cinch for
the pennant.

"How'd you like Squill? What a second sacker! That
kid's another Eddie Collins! He'll give us the best infield outside the big leagues!"

Kearns nodded his head. "He's good! Got more hustle
than anybody I ever saw."

"You oughta seen him when I had him. Duer don't

know how to handle him, wants to get rid of him. I heard some of the Parkville fans talkin' about the trouble him and Duer's been havin' and that means we can get him cheap."

"Could be," Kearns murmured dryly, "but you can bet your life Eddie Duer won't break up his infield until the season's over. Let's forget trades and players and everything for now except the pennant. I'm sure glad, as it turned out, that we were rained out of those early games with the Bears."

"Me too!" Breen agreed. "Those rain checks are gonna mean the pennant for us as sure as shootin'!"

Eddie Duer had no idea what Kearns and Breen were talking about but, right then, he was thinking the same thing. But for the early season rain, these last three defeats by the Mules wouldn't have been possible. Dressing slowly, he was thinking back through the season when his youngsters had been burning up the league, had owned the Mules. Now, the shoe was on the other foot and he was worried sick. The sudden surge of the Mules and their surprising domination of his team was puzzling. He knew a change of managers often resulted in a sudden lift in the spirit and play of a club, but he couldn't understand why it should affect another club's play, especially his club. But it had. There was no getting around it. The Bears had lost their confidence where the Mules were concerned.

Chip sensed that, too. The Bears were a whipped club in spirit and in fact. He glanced cautiously around the room, noting the subdued voices and the absence of the usual banter and boisterous needling. And, on the train that night, the team talk centered around one subject— the Mules.

"Don't get it! Some of those guys can't hit the size of their hats yet they knock us out of the park."

"Been teeing off the last three games!"

"Something's wrong!"

"Well, we won't get anywhere lookin' over our shoulders," Eddie Duer remarked pointedly. "What's done is done. Let's take the Wasps tomorrow and then think about the Mules."

The Bears took the Wasps, all right, sending three chuckers to the showers and pounding out an 11 to 3 win. Their spirits rose sharply, too, when the lowly Comets took the overconfident Mules, 2 to 1. That increased their lead to three and a half games and put all the burden of winning the pennant on the Mules.

Chip had concentrated on Corky Squill and he was more puzzled than ever. Because Squill had made a complete about-face, had retreated once more into his shell. And he remained in his shell during the Monday practice, sphinxlike in his play and in his behavior toward his teammates.

The Parkville fans were up in arms and out in force to help their beloved Bears meet the Mules' pennant threat Tuesday afternoon. This three-game series here in the home-town park was the crucial series. The Bears had five more games to play, all with the Mules. The Mules had six games to play. The pennant could be won in the next two days!

Chip slipped away when Kildane was surrounded by a group of admiring fans outside the ball park and hurried to a ticket window. He had a little difficulty but finally got a seat right behind the plate. That seat was his destination when, just before game time, he moved unobtrusively out of the dugout and through the gate leading to the stands. Most of the fans knew him and several spoke to him. Chip felt embarrassed in the grandstand wearing a uniform and almost turned back.

But he was determined to check something once and for all and the seat behind the plate was important.

Eddie Duer started Windy Mills, and the Mules started swinging from their heels with the first pitch. And the Bears didn't get them out until four runs had scored and Mills was under the shower. Akers relieved Mills with two down and the bases loaded, but only a storybook up-against-the-fence catch by Ted Smith in right field saved the day.

Chip was concentrating on Corky Squill every second that the Bears were in the field. It required concentration, all right, for Corky was again a human dynamo, pepping it up and hustling and moving back and forth continuously, or so it seemed to Chip. Innings later, in the confusion of the home-team stretch and with the Mules leading 8 to 0, Chip made his way through the standing fans and back into the dugout. He hadn't even been missed. Chip was glad of that, for he thought he knew at last the reason why the Parkville hurlers couldn't get the visitors out. He'd know for sure tomorrow.

The Parkville fans weren't worried, but their pride was hurt by the ease with which the Mules were handling their heroes. The Mules had now won four in a row from the Bears. It didn't figure.

"We'll take 'em tomorrow, all right!"

"We'd have the pennant won if Kildane hadn't been hurt!"

"Something funny about that deal. Never did hear the real story of how he got hurt!"

"You, nor no one else," someone observed. "I think Eddie Duer ruined his arm, used him too much—"

The Bear players began to show the effects of the strain, too. The 8–0 lacing that afternoon had added to

the tension which was building up so steadily and, like
the fans, they began to think what might have been,
how the pennant might have been all wrapped up if
Scissors Kildane had been available. Not that they
doubted their ability to take the series and with it the
pennant, but the Mules seemed to be getting all the
breaks.

But they were whistling in the dark. Each was as
tight as a drum. Wednesday afternoon brought disaster.
That is, to the Parkville fans and the Bears. For the
Mules did it again! The pennant-hungry invaders un-
leashed a savage hitting attack which drove every available Bear chucker to the showers and accounted for
nine runs while the home-town forces could muster only
three scattered tallies. That cut the Parkville lead a full
game and, for the first time, the confidence of the Bear
fans, the players, and Eddie Duer was shaken.

Chip Hilton's confidence was shaken, too. Once again
he had slipped out of the dugout and had watched the
game from the grandstand. And what he had seen convinced him that he held the key to the Mules domination of the Bears' pitching.

Scissors Kildane wasn't very talkative that night at
dinner and toyed with his dessert until only he and
Chip remained in the room. It was just as well because
Chip was deeply involved in his problem. No matter
how he tried, he always came back to Kildane. He decided to get it off his chest.

"Scissors," he began slowly, "could we sit in the
grandstand tomorrow during the game?"

Kildane looked at him in surprise. "In the grandstand," he repeated. "Heck, no, Chip. I've gotta stay
with the team. This is the stretch and I belong in the
bull pen."

"You can do more in the grandstand, Scissors. Look,

I've got two tickets right behind the plate. You sit with me for two or three innings and you'll learn something important."

"Like what?"

"Like why the Mules hit so well against us."

Kildane stared at Chip in surprise. "What's the grandstand got to do with it?"

"Well, for one thing you can tell whether or not I'm right when I call the pitches."

"Call the pitches," Kildane echoed. "You mean you can call the pitch before Akers and Mills and Richards and the rest of us throw?"

"I think I can. I called them yesterday and today."

Kildane's eyes widened in astonishment. But behind the shock of surprise his mind was working with lightning speed. Disbelief had been the first reaction, but he had come to know Chip Hilton. He knew his young friend to be a clear thinker, unlikely to make such a statement unless he was sure of his ground.

"How? How can you tell?"

"I'd rather not say, Scissors."

"But if you can call the pitch, Chip, why maybe someone else can, too. Maybe the Mules can tell! They sure act as though they know what we're going to throw. Come on! We gotta see Eddie!"

But Chip wasn't going to be rushed into that position. He shook his head vigorously. "I won't tell Mr. Duer anything, Scissors. I'd tell you first, if I was going to tell anyone. I can prove it's possible, but you'll have to figure the rest out yourself."

"But why, Chip? S'pose the Mules know! Why they'll win every game, might knock us out of the pennant!"

But Chip was adamant. He wasn't going to tell anyone what he suspected. Even if he knew for a certainty he was right he wouldn't tell.

CHAPTER 15

DOUBLE-CROSS SIGNS

SCISSORS KILDANE in the grandstand! That was something! The lucky fans who surrounded the popular chucker had recognized him immediately, greeting him with affection and enthusiasm.

"Hey! Scissors! How come?"

"How you feelin'? We gonna take 'em today?"

"Who's working? How's the ribs?"

"Hiya, Hilton. How ya doin'?"

Kildane was everybody's pal and he had an answer for every question, but he didn't neglect the business at hand. His midnight talk with Eddie Duer had been lengthy and thorough. The worried manager had been doubtful but he wasn't overlooking the possibility that Chip had struck pay dirt.

"Chip's a smart youngster, Scissors, and he may have caught something we've overlooked. You know, there's something gosh-awful funny about the way the Mules have been teeing off on us."

"You're telling me!" Kildane said wryly.

"Anyway," Duer continued, "there's nothing to lose, and if Chip's been clever enough to figure it out, let's play along. Okay?"

It had been more than "okay" with Kildane. If finding the answer to the humiliation he had suffered from the Mules' bats meant walking from Parkville to Hedgetown on his knees, Scissors Kildane was all for it. So, appearing to be without a care in the world, he responded gaily to the fans but he concentrated upon Chip Hilton.

Softy Richards was clever. He knew all the tricks in the bag. His delivery was as tricky as his stock in trade, and his all-time record against the Mules stood at nine wins against two defeats. But today something was wrong. When he bent one, the hitter stepped into it, met the ball before the break. When he fired a fast one, the batter leveled off, swung from the dugout. Softy couldn't understand it nor could the fans.

Eddie Duer knew the Mule hitters about as well as his own, knew the type of pitch they liked and those they didn't. Mickey Curry knew the Mules just as well and worked Richards perfectly. But it was no use and the frustration in the glance he directed at Duer each time he hustled into the dugout expressed his feelings better than words.

Back of the plate, in the grandstand, a shocked and incredulous Scissors Kildane heard Chip call every pitch as accurately as if he could read Mickey Curry's mind. Curry would squat, flash the signs to Richards, and right then, almost as quickly, Chip would whisper "fast ball" or "hook" or "change-up," as the case might be.

Kildane checked each pitch and then tried to figure it out. He knew it was a waste of time, but he checked Curry, anyway. The veteran receiver never varied his procedure, gave the signs with the fingers of his meat hand pressed closely against the inside of his right leg in the squat. And when he fixed his big glove as a target it was always held in the same position.

"Nope," Kildane muttered, "it isn't Mickey. It's gotta be Richards!"

But it wasn't Richards. At least Kildane could detect no giveaway in Softy's delivery. In desperation, he checked the houses beyond the center-field fence, half expecting to see, even at that distance, someone with a pair of binoculars and a mirror flashing the signs. It was an extreme thought but he was at his wit's end, determined to check every possibility. But it was no go and Kildane finally admitted that he was completely baffled.

"I don't get it, Chip. Look, you've just gotta tell me. This is serious."

"I'm sorry, Scissors. I can't tell you—I just can't!"

"But this is murder, Chip. If you can get the signs they can too—unless you're a mind reader."

"I'm no mind reader, and there's nothing particularly mysterious about it, Scissors. Nothing you can't figure out."

"How about Breen, Chip? He's in the coaching box. He got anything to do with it? You can tell me that much."

Chip deliberated briefly, then nodded. "Yes, he has, Scissors," he said firmly. "A lot to do with it. But that's all I'm going to say."

Kildane studied Chip with a long, penetrating glance. Then he nodded his head understandingly. "I get it, Chip," he said softly. "You're right! You're absolutely right. I won't bother you any more about it. I think I know, now, why you can't tell me. Look. You stay right here. I've got to talk to Eddie. Okay?"

Kildane didn't pause to talk to the fans. He hurried down the steps and through the gate next to the dugout. A despairing glance at the scoreboard told him that it was too late to do much about this game. It was the bottom of the eighth and the Mules were out in front, 11 to 2. But he could at least tell Duer that Breen was getting the signs some way.

Eddie Duer hadn't given up. The fighting manager of the Bears was driving his players by word and example. He talked confidently to his faltering youngsters, aggressively demanding that they go get him some runs.

"Come on. Let's get on this guy! Where's the life in this dugout? What's a few runs! Come on, Bucky, start it off!"

But the Bears couldn't get started, didn't even reach first. And it didn't really matter that the Mules got two more runs in the top of the ninth, for the Bears were blanked again in their last time at bat. So, the Mules swept the series and cut the Bears' lead to half a game. That left the Mules with three games to play, one with the Comets and the two final games of the season with the Bears at Hedgetown.

It had been a tragic series for the Bears and the Parkville fans. The three-and-a-half-game lead had looked big three days ago. Now it had practically vanished and anything could happen, especially in the final two-game series at Hedgetown.

Scissors Kildane hadn't lost any time in reporting his grandstand experience, excitedly whispering the details to Eddie Duer while the Bears were in the field in the top of the ninth.

"Can't be," Duer said doubtfully. "Chip knows our signs, so what?"

"Sure, we all know them, Eddie, but you can't see 'em up in the stands!"

"Holy socks! You're right! I never thought of that! How in the world does he do it?"

"Only way I can see is that he knows by the motions," Kildane said ruefully. "Mine too, I guess."

Duer nodded thoughtfully. "Could be, but you know what that means? If Chip can figure our chuckers, so can Gabby Breen and everyone else in the league. Particularly Gabby Breen!"

"Chip calls every pitch, Eddie. I know it sounds fishy, but it's true. He called them before the windup, and if he said 'fast ball,' fast ball it was. And when he said 'hook,' it was a hook! Heck, I checked every pitch—not just a few."

"And he wouldn't say how he could tell?"

"Nothing, except that Breen was mixed up in it."

"You watch Breen?"

"Sure, but he wasn't doing anything unusual that I could see. He was giving signals to their hitters and runners just like we do."

"You think he could see Mickey's signs?"

"No! Positively not! Heck, he didn't even seem to be looking at the plate when Mickey was giving his signs."

Duer shook his head worriedly. "Well, we're sure gonna do something about it soon as this debacle is over. Nothing like this ever happened to me in all the years I've been in baseball."

Right after the game, Duer headed for Bill Malloy's stadium office, leaving Bob Reiter to bring Mickey Curry and Scissors Kildane upstairs as soon as possible.

To say that Bill Malloy was shocked by Eddie Duer's disclosure was putting it mildly. Malloy had been in baseball a long time, never as a player but as an enthusiastic patron of the sport. When the first shock of surprise wore off he began a cold analysis of the situation.

"It makes sense, Eddie!" Malloy declared. "The Mules have taken us six in a row and, whether it's a coincidence or not, every one of those lickings has occurred since Gabby Breen took over."

"Lickings is right," Duer echoed sourly. "We haven't given them a close game in a month."

"Of course," Malloy deliberated, "the boy could know Kildane and Richards and Mills and the rest of them so well that he might be able to figure out the pitch, especially if he knew the play situation and the hitters' weaknesses."

"But he said Breen was in the picture."

"That could be his own imagination. Breen undoubtedly flashes hit-and-take signs to each batter and Hilton may have picked those up."

"Could be," Duer agreed doubtfully, "but Scissors said he called every pitch, never missed on a single one."

"Doesn't seem possible. Why don't we get the boy up here?"

"Scissors said he clammed up, wouldn't say how he could call the pitches nor anything else, except that Breen was the key. He'd confide in Scissors before anyone else. The two kids are firm friends and you can bet he'd tell Scissors if he was going to tell. Hilton's a sensitive kid and we've got to remember his position. He's more or less an outsider, can't be expected to horn in."

"I guess you're right. Anyway, he's given us plenty to work on and we ought to be able to carry the ball from here. S'pose we leave his name out of our discussion with Reiter and Curry. You think Scissors told them anything?"

Duer shook his head. "No, I told Scissors not to breathe a word to anyone."

"Good! We can keep Scissors out of it, too. He's clever, he'll understand."

"You can be sure of that. Another thing, if we keep the two of them out of it maybe Hilton will open up. He's s'posed to go home Saturday night to get ready to go to college."

Malloy nodded. "We've got a job cut out for us, all right. If the Mules win tomorrow and there's no reason to think they won't, we'll be all tied up."

"Yeah, and trying to win those two games at Hedgetown will be like robbing Fort Knox!"

"Well, we've got to figure out how they're getting the signs and we'll sure have to change them."

Their conversation was interrupted by the arrival of Bob Reiter with Scissors Kildane and Mickey Curry in tow. The three men entered the office uncertainly and a trifle awkwardly. But Bill Malloy immediately put them at their ease, smiling warmly as he shook hands with each player.

"Sit down, men. Sorry to hold you up, but we're in the middle of something important. Eddie, s'pose you bring things up to date."

Eddie Duer's words hit Bob Reiter and Mickey Curry like a bombshell. Scissors Kildane knew what was coming.

"Fellows," Duer said grimly, "the Mules have been getting our signs!"

Varied emotions were expressed upon the faces of each of Duer's listeners. Bill Malloy's eyes ranged from one face to another as he noted their reactions. Bob Reiter was nonplused. He shook his head in astonishment. Mickey Curry's eyes blinked furiously and little knots of muscles gathered about his tightly clamped jaws. Then he nodded his head vigorously.

"I knew it!" he said through tightly pressed lips. "Had to be! Their hitters were set for every pitch!"

Bob Reiter's speech came back in a rush of words.

"No wonder we couldn't get 'em out! I couldn't figure it, couldn't figure guys like Conover and Roth and Kinkaid lacin' the ball every time they come up."

"An' Berry and Baker," Curry added.

"Well, even I could hit if I knew every pitch that was coming," Duer said ruefully.

"How they gettin' the signs?" Curry asked. "Heck, I know they aren't getting 'em from me. Why, I've even been wearing an inner shirt with long sleeves so the muscles on my forearm wouldn't show when I gave the signs."

"That's nonsense!" Reiter exploded. "I never did believe a coach could steal signs by watching the muscles in a catcher's arm."

"It's not nonsense!" Duer said sharply. "We can't overlook a single possibility. The Mules are getting the signs and it means the pennant unless we can check it."

"But how?" Curry insisted. "How they getting them and how do we know they're getting them?"

"We don't know how they're getting them, Mickey," Duer explained, "but you can take my word that they're getting every sign we throw. And if we don't check it, we can kiss the pennant good-bye."

"Well, what's the next move?" Reiter asked. "What do we do now?"

"Change the signs for one thing," Curry said quickly.

"Maybe that won't be enough," Duer said meaningly, wishing he didn't have to say the words.

A long silence followed, each person in the room reluctantly exploring the possibilities the statement implied.

Bill Malloy brought them relief from that repugnant thought. The owner of the Bears wasn't ready to accept that implication. "Changing the signs will be enough, Eddie," he said assuringly. "You'd better work up two

sets and check every possible leak. You can do a lot between now and Saturday."

"I'll have to!" Duer said shortly.

"You using me Saturday, Eddie?" Kildane asked
quietly. "That's the big one and Doc said I was ready
to go."

"You're sure right, Scissors," Duer said grimly. "It's
the big one—and you're pitching!"

CHAPTER 16

TRIPLE JEOPARDY

EDDIE DUER didn't wait until the next day to work out a new set of signs. He got busy that night. Nine o'clock found Reiter, Curry, and Kildane in Duer's room and no time was lost in getting started.

"We'll hold skull practice tomorrow morning in the clubhouse at ten o'clock, Bob," Duer said briskly, "and in the afternoon we'll work behind closed gates."

Reiter nodded approvingly. "How about the train?"

"Right! Pulls out at six-fifty and we can work in my compartment."

"That train's gonna be jammed with fans," Curry warned.

Duer glanced sharply at Reiter. "You see Pepper and tell him to get on the job. I don't want anyone in our car except the team, Mr. Malloy, and Chip Hilton. Understand? Okay, now let's get busy."

Mickey Curry was an ideal leader. He was an experienced catcher, a fighter, and a team player. And, as the person chiefly responsible for the signs, it was only natural that he should take the lead in making suggestions. He leaned forward, now, speaking earnestly in his soft voice.

167

"We've been using two sets, Eddie. Maybe we ought to try an addition series and start our signs at six. That way, six would be a fast ball, seven a hook, eight the change-up, and nine a pitchout."

"Might be okay," Duer agreed. "That means you can call for a fast ball several ways. You can flash three fingers twice or two fingers three times, right?"

"Too complicated," Reiter said worriedly. "We don't have many Einsteins."

"It's got to be complicated," Curry interrupted. "I've been working behind the bat for twelve years and this is the first time I ever had trouble with the signs. If they're getting the signs in spite of the way I've been protecting them—well, the more complicated the better."

Duer settled the issue. "We'll use Mickey's addition series," he said flatly. "Mickey, you work with the chuckers. Bob, you take Corky and Bucky.

"Another thing, Bob, I want you to check up on the way Corky and Bucky flash the signs to the outfield. Get it? And while you're at it, you'd better check the outfielders. Maybe Dawson or Klein or Smith are shifting some way on the relay or using some sort of a motion.

"I know all this seems extreme but with the championship at stake, and, in view of what we know, we can't afford to overlook a single possibility. Now, you fellows put on your thinking caps and check whether or not we've overlooked anything. Mickey, I want you and Scissors to stay here a little while longer. The rest of you can go."

Duer sat quietly after the others had left, looking from Scissors to Curry. Then he got up and locked the door, checked the transom, lowered the two windows, and then sat down on the bed. His whole manner was secretive and when he spoke it was in a near-whisper.

"I hope what I'm about to talk over with you two fellows will never be repeated and never have to be used. But, as I said before, no possibility can be overlooked and it may be necessary for us to disregard *all* team signs."

Curry was bewildered. "You mean you think someone—"

"I mean that there's too much at stake to overlook *any* possibilities," Duer said firmly. "I want you two fellows to have a special set of signs of your own."

"That means two sets at one time, then," Curry said doubtfully. "One for the team and another for me and Scissors."

"Any other ideas?" Duer asked.

"Why can't I flash the signs for the hitter and have Mickey give the team signs?" Kildane queried.

"That would be better," Curry agreed. "Heck, Scissors flashed 'em to me in several games last year and I relayed them to the gang. It'll work better if we have to use two sets."

"Maybe," Duer said thoughtfully. "But what about the other fellows? They'll be playing for one pitch and Scissors will be throwing another. Maybe it would be better if you didn't give any signs at all, Mickey. Yes, I think that's better. If things come to a showdown, we'll cut out all team signs and let Scissors flash his own just to you. Well, thanks, boys, that's all. Get a good night's sleep."

Chip spent a lonely evening. It was the first time he had been entirely on his own since he had joined the Bears. He walked aimlessly about the streets for a while, finally ending up in a movie. But he didn't enjoy the picture, his mind was too filled with thoughts of the race and the signs and of home. This time Saturday night he'd be on his way back to Valley Falls. Then, after a week at home, he'd be off to college. Off to State and football.

Kildane was in bed when Chip got back to the hotel, but he wasn't asleep. The lanky chucker was thinking about the big game on Saturday and the signs and he wanted to talk.

"Snap on the light, Chip, I wasn't asleep. Where'd you go? Show? Boy, this has been a long day. You know, I still can't figure out how you can call the signs. Sure wish you'd tell. It would certainly save me a lot of brainwork."

Chip shook his head. He hadn't changed his mind on that score and he wasn't going to change it. Kildane sighed and tried another angle.

"You sure you have to leave Saturday night? Can't you wait until Sunday?"

"I can't stay, Scissors. I shouldn't have stuck around this long. I'll sure be listening on the radio, though."

Chip wished he was listening on the radio the next morning. Wished he was far away from Eddie Duer and the Bear players who were gathered in the clubhouse and who were thunderstruck by the manager's revelation concerning the signs.

"Boys, the Mules are getting our signs. That's why they've been able to hit us so freely the last couple weeks. And one thing's sure—they're stealing the signs or someone's tipping them off."

There was a deep silence as the impact of the ugly thought struck home. After a moment, Duer continued. "I'll rule the second part out right now. I know every player on this ball club and I'd trust every one of you with my life. But they're getting them, so that means they're stealing them.

"The only thing we can do is to use two or three sets

of signs. Starting tomorrow, we'll use different signs all through the game, maybe change every inning."

That afternoon, for the first time since Eddie Duer took over as the Parkville manager, the Bear workout was private, held behind locked gates. Two or three hundred boosters had shown up and had expressed keen disappointment at the sudden change of policy but you would never have known they were disgruntled had you seen them that evening at the depot. For everyone in town knew by that time that the Mules had white-washed the Comets 6 to 0 at Alton and that the race was all tied up with two games to go. That was the reason the huge crowd was on hand to cheer the Bears and to try to get aboard the six-fifty.

"Sure I know there's a special train! But I want to ride with the team!"

"Tickets? What tickets? I'll pay cash!"

"But you can't put me off, I *have* a ticket!"

"Yes, they are aboard! They've got a special car right back there on the rear end!"

The last fan was right. The official Bear party had been ushered through the crowd and back to the end of the train to a special car. But several thousand frenzied fans were surging around the end of the train and the majority of the Parkville rooters caught only a glimpse of their heroes waving from the windows and from the rear platform as the train left the station.

When the bus pulled away from the hotel the next morning at eleven o'clock, Chip found himself beside William Malloy. And when Scissors Kildane toed the rubber and faced the first Mule hitter in the bottom half of the initial inning, the owner of the Bears was still beside him—in the grandstand directly back of home plate.

"Chip, you don't have to tell me a thing," Malloy explained, "I just want to hear you call the pitches. I just can't believe it."

Chip could call the pitches and did, calling them correctly every time. Malloy was flabbergasted. And down on the field, Mickey Curry and Scissors Kildane were just as confused. For the hits were ringing off the Mules' bats as though it was batting practice. The first three Mule hitters had singled and the bases were loaded.

Chip had never been in the middle of a crowd like this one. Every person there was on his feet and the crowd roar was like the thunder of a hundred Niagara Falls. And about all of the words a fellow could distinguish were concerned with Scissors Kildane.

Eddie Duer had called "time" and was talking to Kildane and Curry in front of the mound.

"You all right, Scissors? You sure you're all right?"

"I'm right, Eddie! I never felt better in my life!"

Curry agreed. "He's okay, Skipper, but it looks like they're still at it. They're set for everything he throws."

Duer shook his head grimly. "Well, change the signs again, that's all I know to do."

The plate umpire touched Duer with the mask he held in his hand. "Time, Eddie," he said. "Play ball!"

"Play ball! Play ball!" roared out from the stands. "Play ball!"

Duer glanced at the runners perched on the bases and then at Fellows, the Mules' big first sacker. It was a tough spot. Fellows could hit the long ball.

Fellows did hit the long ball! One of the longest ever seen in Hedgetown! He met Kildane's fast ball right on the nose and the horsehide sailed high over and beyond the left-field wall. It was a grand slam blow, a homer in any park in the land, and the Mules were way out in front with four runs across and no one out.

That did it! Duer barked "time" and was out of the dugout like a shot, his face an angry red. He motioned to Curry and Kildane and waved the others away. "All right, Scissors, you're giving your own signs. Curry, you shake him off if you don't like 'em, but don't give any signs. This has gone far enough!"

Bill Malloy was of the same opinion. He knew, now, that Duer had been right. Someone was giving the signs away and if Chip Hilton could call the pitches, why couldn't the Mules? He rose abruptly and started for the dugout, fighting his way through the hysterical mob. By the time he reached the dugout, Conover had walked, Roth had sacrificed the runner to second, and Kildane was pitching to Kinkaid.

"You're right," Malloy puffed, dropping heavily down on the bench beside Duer. "Right as daylight! The kid called every shot. I thought you changed the signs."

"Did! Put in an addition set, too! But you saw what happened."

"Scissors right?"

"Mickey says he was never better."

"What you doin' about the signs, now?"

"Kildane's giving his own. Maybe that will—"

Duer never finished that sentence, for Kinkaid had just met one on the nose and Conover came tearing in from third. Kinkaid had always been pie and ice cream for Kildane, for the whole Bear pitching staff so far as that was concerned. But he had chosen this particular situation to prove that the exception makes the rule by swinging from his heels and meeting the full-count fast ball dead center with the meat of the bat. The ball hadn't been hit hard but it had been hit right, had carried all the way to the fence in right center. Kinkaid slid safely into third just ahead of Klein's peg. That made it 5 to 0, with a man on third, one down, and Bingo Berry at bat.

Kildane was desperate. He had never experienced anything like this and he decided to pitch to the Mules as if he had never faced them before. That was the reason he surprised Curry by resorting to the sole use of his fast ball. And he surprised Bingo Berry, too. Berry liked a fast ball, letter high, and Kildane gave it to him right through the middle for a called strike. And he came right back with another and then another. Berry got a piece of the first one but he missed the next one a country mile for the out.

Skids Baker came sauntering out to the mound and the thunder from the stands was deafening. But the fireball chucker couldn't handle his own stock in trade, the fast ball. Kildane's hard one was jumping and Baker went down swinging on three dazzling streaks of light which split the plate.

The Bears came hustling in, but they were worried. They couldn't understand what was happening. Bucky Boyd grabbed Curry by the arm. "What goes with the signs?" he demanded.

"You keepin' 'em secret?" Squill barked. "What are we s'posed to do? Guess what Kildane's gonna throw?"

"Ask Eddie," Curry said shortly. "It's his orders!"

Duer sprang up out of the dugout, nodding soberly as the players faced around. "That's right," he said evenly, "it's my orders. They're still getting the signs, so Scissors is flashing 'em to Curry and the rest of you are on your own."

The statement was received in dead silence. Dismay was in the eyes of most of them, and the surprise and

shock was so great that they forgot it was their turn at
bat. They were roused into action only by the plate
umpire's raucous "Play ball!"

"Play ball!" came rolling down from the stands as the
Hedgetown fans exulted in the pennant surge of the
Mules. But the Bears seemed to have lost all desire to
play ball. They were shocked, barely went through the
motions. A player had to be "up" when he was playing
a clutch game in a tight pennant race. Way up! But a
fellow couldn't fight when his confidence in his own
teammates was shattered.

Bucky Boyd and Paul Hale exchanged long bewildered glances, and Norman Klein and Stretch Johnson moved away from the bat rack as if they were walking on stilts. Klein knelt in the on-deck circle and leaned
on his bat. But he didn't address Johnson in his usual
cheery manner. He didn't yell "Get on, Stretch. I'll
bring you in!" No, Klein was looking down at the
ground trying to figure it all out.

Stretch Johnson, batting lefty, cast a quick glance at
the dugout, then at Eddie Duer in the third-base coaching box, and stepped slowly up to the plate. Johnson's
arms felt lifeless, drained of all their strength. He swung
that way, too. Three times. When the inning ended, the
fans almost kicked down the stands as they cheered
Skids Baker for his three straight strike-outs, and the
Bears walked out to their positions a beaten team.

The less said about that game, if game one could
call it, the better. The Mules whitewashed the Bears
9 to 0. That put Hedgetown out in front in the pennant
race with one game to go, sure of a tie in the final
standings and, judging by the play of the Bears, a
shoo-in for the pennant.

Yes, it looked bad for the Bears. Several thousand

Hedgetown fans made sure the Parkville heroes were advised of that fact. They were packed in a solid mass from the players' gate to the Bears' bus.

"What happened to Kildane?"

"You guys gonna show up tomorrow?"

"One down and one to go and you guys ain't goin' anywhere."

"You kissed the pennant good-bye today, fellas. If Kildane couldn't do it, no one can."

"Didn't have it in the clutch, didya? Ya bums!"

"Just a bunch of front runners, that's all!"

CHAPTER 17

A GREAT COMEBACK

BILL MALLOY had watched his team go to pieces that afternoon and he knew it would take superhuman effort to pull the pieces together. The Bears had been a team until that fateful first inning. Following that disastrous start and Duer's abrupt announcement that the signs were out, that the team was on its own and Scissors Kildane was giving his own signs, the team of talented youngsters had changed to a collection of individual stars playing pickup ball. And pickup ball wasn't going to beat the Mules the way they were going. That was the reason Malloy followed the players to the clubhouse and the reason Eddie Duer called them together after they had showered and dressed.

"Men," Malloy began, "this is the first time this year I've felt it was necessary for me to talk to you about your play on the field." He gestured toward Duer. "Eddie is a great manager, has my full confidence, and I know he understands that I am taking this step only because I feel it is necessary."

The Bears shifted uneasily in their seats, wondering what was coming next. After a brief pause, Malloy continued. "I saw a great team fall apart this afternoon. I

saw a bunch of kids who had banded themselves together with tremendous fighting spirit suddenly lose all
their poise and hustle. And I know why! Because they
lost confidence in one another.

"You men forged to the top of the Midwestern League
to the surprise of everyone except Eddie Duer and myself. Eddie and I knew you had it! We know you still
have it, have what it takes to come back and win the
pennant. Tomorrow's game is a must! It has to be won!
But it isn't going to be won unless we can regain our
team spirit. That's what we have to do tonight!

"I've asked Eddie to call a meeting for nine o'clock. I
want every player there because we're going to decide
upon a set of signs and we're going to use them tomorrow. Win, lose, or draw! Not only for the catcher and
the pitcher but for the team—just as we've used them
all year."

Chip listened with varied emotions. Changing the
signs wouldn't be any good as long as Corky Squill was
giving them away. Why, they could change the signs
every pitch and Squill could still give them away. Chip
glanced at the doughty second baseman. Squill was
completely ensconced in his shell, looking straight
ahead. Corky was a hard nut to crack, difficult to figure
out.

Two hours later Chip began packing his suitcase. He
folded the Bear uniform carefully and spread it on the
bed. Despite his protests, Eddie Duer had made him
take it, had patted him on the shoulder and said, "We
want you to have it, Chip. Just as a souvenir, even if
you never wear it again."

He'd wear it all right, Chip was thinking. Be proud
of it as long as he lived. Chip wished he could stay for
the last game . . . that was going to be something to
see. But he had to go home as he had planned.

He smoothed out the uniform and walked over to the window. He was lonesome and there was a heaviness in his chest which wouldn't go away. He could still feel the friendly handclasps of Scissors and Duer and Bill Malloy and Mickey Curry when they had said good-bye. They sure were a great bunch . . . didn't deserve to lose the pennant because of trickery or deceit. . . .

Chip glanced at his watch. He still had an hour to kill. So he sat down on the bed and tried to figure out what he ought to do about Corky Squill. Duer and Scissors and Mickey Curry were together right at that moment trying to dope out a new set of signs. They wanted to have them all set before the team meeting. Chip didn't think Duer and Kildane or Curry would be able to do anything about the signs and there didn't seem to be much he could do about it either. Time was running out. He wished Kildane could have gone to the train with him. Maybe he could have given Scissors a better lead.

Chip's thoughts swung to Valley Falls. This time tomorrow he'd be home. But, before he got aboard that train, something had to be done about Corky Squill. Someone had to talk to Corky and he was the only person to do it.

Gabby Breen wanted to talk to Corky Squill, too. The scrappy infielder was very much in the Mule manager's thoughts. Breen had been thrilled by the big win which put the Mules in the lead, but he had been worried sick for eight solid innings. Something had gone wrong and the wily manager wanted to be sure it was straightened out before the final game. He watched the clock and fretted and fussed and paced the floor. Eventually he began to talk out loud, voicing his thoughts.

"Wonder what happened? Good thing we got those five runs in the first inning! Broke their backs! Gotta be sure about tomorrow! Everything's gotta click! Just gotta! How about a team trailin' the whole season and then goin' out in front in the next to the last game? Bet Eddie Duer ain't feelin' so hot tonight! Hope he feels the same way tomorrow night. Why doesn't that little punk call? Shootin' his mouth off somewhere. I s'pose!"

Corky Squill wasn't "shootin' his mouth off." He was listening. Listening to Chip Hilton. Chip had located Squill in the lobby, waiting for the nine-o'clock meeting. The lone wolf was nervous, and just when Chip thought he might have to face Squill right there in front of the others, the lonesome second baseman sauntered out the front door and down the street. Chip followed, catching up with Squill near the middle of the block.

"Could I talk with you a minute, Corky?"

Squill faced around in startled surprise. "What's that?" he demanded truculently. "What did you say?"

"I said I'd like to talk to you about the signs," Chip said evenly.

Squill's eyes narrowed and he moved a step nearer to Chip, measuring the distance to the youngster's chin. "Signs?" he echoed, lowering his voice. "What signs?"

"The team signs," Chip said patiently. "The signs for the pitcher."

Squill's eyes glittered angrily. He clenched his fists and expanded his chest. "Look, Hilton," he grated, "I don't want to talk to you about anything! Period! All I want to do is hang one on your chin!"

"Would you rather I told Eddie Duer?"

"What do I care who you tell? I don't know what you're talkin' about."

"I'm talking about the way you give away the signs."

"*I* give away the signs," Squill growled, moving forward. "Why you—"

"Just a second, Corky," Chip said calmly. "You give away the signs for every pitch. I've been in the stands for the past two games and I called every pitch—just by watching you. And if I can call them by watching you, so can Gabby Breen!"

Squill's face was contorted with rage and he was on the verge of lashing out at the boy facing him. "What's that," he asked, checked by the mention of Gabby Breen. "You can call the signs by watchin' me?"

"That's right!"

"You're nuts!"

"Not quite. Now listen—"

Squill listened while Chip described every move Corky made in the field and explained its relation to the pitch. As Chip talked, he watched Squill warily, prepared for the worst. But the infielder's face was a blank, only his glittering eyes showing his intense interest.

"Every time Curry signals for a fast ball to a right-handed hitter you move two or three steps to the left and back," said Chip, watching Squill intently. "All Breen has to do is to see your move and pass the information on to his hitter from the third-base coaching box. When a fast ball is to be pitched to a left-handed hitter, you take two or three steps to the right and back, don't you, Corky? And when Curry signals for a curve or slider—do you want me to go on, Corky?"

A bewildered Corky eyed Chip ominously at the end. Standing there with his hands on his hips, he coldly appraised the tall youngster he called the jinx.

"You're a pretty smart apple, aren't you?" he said bitterly. "Pretty smart. You say anything to anyone else about this?"

"No, not with respect to your part in it. I told Scissors I could call the pitches and proved it and I did the same with Mr. Malloy, but I didn't tell them how I could do it."

"And you didn't tell a single soul you were watchin' me?"

"No."

Squill's eyes drilled Chip through and through as he searched the face of the boy. "Why not?" he asked suddenly and sharply. "Why didn't you spill it?"

"Because I don't play ball that way, Corky. I couldn't! Well, I've got to catch my train. I'm sorry we couldn't be friends, Corky, and I'm sorry about the signs."

"Just a minute," Squill said quickly. "How come you're tellin' me all this now?"

"Because I'm hoping you can do something about it before tomorrow's game."

"And you ain't gonna tell anyone else?"

Chip shook his head. "No, Corky," he said firmly, "I'm not going to tell anyone anything—ever. Now, I've got to hurry or I'll miss my train."

Squill watched Chip hurry into the hotel and he was standing in the same spot when Chip emerged a few minutes later. Chip lifted his arm in a farewell gesture, but Squill never moved. After Chip's cab pulled away, Squill walked slowly down the street to the corner cigar store, entered a telephone booth, and called Gabby Breen.

Breen was waiting and grabbed the receiver before the end of the first ring. "Hello, Corky. Sure glad you called. Was getting worried. . . . It wasn't your fault! The rest of them bums quit! All but Kildane. Well, tomorrow's another day. . . . Hope not! Say, Kearns said I was to contact Duer soon as it's over and whaddaya think? He wants me to talk trades with Eddie and you're the man he wants! I told you it would work out, didn't I? . . . He said to go the limit! That means he's sold on you for his field captain. Now, look, Corky. To-morrow's the big day for both of us. Put out for all you're worth. Kearns will be watchin' you the whole game and he'll be imaginin' you in a Mule uniform and playin' for Hedgetown next year. So make it good! Okay?"

Corky Squill passed a fretful night, tossing, turning, and thinking. And Sunday morning brought no relief. That was partly the reason he missed the bus and had to hurry out to the park in a taxi. His teammates were on the field when Squill reached the dressing room. He dressed hurriedly and ran out through the dugout to meet more trouble. Eddie Duer was standing there and gave Squill the bad news.

"You'll be two hundred out in your next pay check, Corky," Duer said coolly, turning abruptly away.

"That's all right," Squill said softly. "Don't worry about it."

Minutes later the players and the fans scrambled to their feet and stood at attention while the strains of "The Star-Spangled Banner" filled the stadium. They listened silently at first, but the lift of the anthem got under their skins and one by one they joined voices un-til it was a mighty chorus. On the last note a great shout went up and the Mules dashed out on the field and Corky Squill sauntered out to the plate. The crucial game was on.

Chip had been glad to get away from the confusion and worry which had been his lot during the hectic days of the past week. He had welcomed the cool comfort of the Pullman car. But his mind had refused to rest. It had carried him right back to Hedgetown, and he was weary and downhearted when he made his way to the dining car in the morning. Eating in a dining car always gave Chip a thrill and he usually tarried as long as possible. But not this morning. Number 12 was rolling right along, and fifteen minutes after he regained his seat in the Pullman, the train slowed down for Valley Falls.

They were all there, just as Chip had expected. Soapy Smith saw him and chased along under his window yelling at the top of his voice. Chip couldn't make out the words but it didn't matter, for ten seconds later he was on the platform and Soapy and Biggie Cohen and Speed Morris and Red Schwartz and Petey Jackson and a dozen other friends were pumping his arms and slapping him on the back and pulling at his coat. Chip greeted them gaily but his eyes searched everywhere until they found her, found his mother waiting at the edge of the noisy group. Chip's heart jumped so violently then that it shut off his breath. But he had enough strength to lift Mary Hilton in his arms and swing her around in the old familiar way. Holding his mother close, Chip forgot he was on the platform, the center of attraction and the target of all eyes. But that wouldn't have mattered to Chip. His mother was first in everything in Chip Hilton's life.

Seconds later, Chip's buddies were at him again, and, with his arm around his mother, he let them pull him along to the street and into Speed Morris' jalopy. Chip and his mother sat beside Speed on the front seat. There, all semblance of order ended. The back seat was a jumble of arms, legs, and bodies, while Biggie, Soapy, and Red sat out in front, on the hood. Yes, they made it and the "old reliable" made it, chugging valiantly along Main Street and eventually to the Hilton residence.

One could have called the roll of the Hilton A.C. right then and there wouldn't have been many absentees. And by two o'clock the missing members had all checked in and had joined Chip in the big living room where the radio was going full blast.

"—Kildane is one of the tallest pitchers in organized baseball, you know. There's the stretch—the pitch—it's in there for a called strike and that's all for the Mules. Now here's Bud Lewis with a message for you fans. Bud—"

Biggie Cohen reached up and clicked off the radio. "Might have a couple cracked ribs but there isn't anything wrong with his arm," he said admiringly.

"That's his twelfth strike-out," Soapy chortled. "Is he hot!"

"No one has reached first yet!"

"Twelve strike-outs in six innings! Wow! Let's see, at that rate he'll have eighteen."

"He can count!"

"And multiply!"

The babble of excited voices gave Chip his first chance to think. His pals had thrown questions at him every minute he had been home and the game had been so exciting he hadn't even thought about the signs. There sure wasn't anything wrong with the signs the Bears were using now. So far, Scissors had held the Mules to one hit while the Bears had driven Baker to the showers and had scored nine runs. Corky Squill had scored three of those runs and had played sensationally in the field. What if he had been wrong about Corky? . . .

Forty minutes later it was all over and the Bears and the Mules had finished the season even Stephen, each with 96 victories and 58 defeats.

"—So that winds it up, ladies and gentlemen. This is George Marsh signing off for Bud Lewis and the Benchley Company. . . ."

"Eleven to one!"

"What a lacing!"

"That means three out of five."

"With the first two games at Hedgetown and the second two at Parkville."

"What if they have to play the fifth game? Where will they play it?"

"Didn't ya hear the guy say the fifth game would be played at Hedgetown?"

"Won't be no fifth game! Won't even be four!" Soapy asserted. "Now that Kildane's back in form!"

Chip grinned. The Hilton A.C. had sure adopted the Bears. He wished he was in the Bears' dressing room right then. It probably was a madhouse.

Chip was right. The Bears' dressing room was, indeed, a madhouse. The players were gleefully turning the room into a shambles. Paul Hale had torn Johnson's straw hat into shreds and the big first sacker had retaliated by forcing the hot-corner guardian under the showers in full uniform. It was glorious fun, a great comeback.

Kildane tried to put through a call on the clubhouse phone but had to give up. The Bears weren't standing for any such nonsense. That was the reason he had to call Chip from the hotel two hours later.

"You get the game, Chip? How'd you like it? . . . Thought I'd call, anyway. Eddie called curfew off and the gang's taking this town apart. . . . Play-off series starts Tuesday. Eddie said he was going to use Richards, but he might change his mind. I've got something important to tell you but I can't do it now. Something about the signs. I'll give you the whole story after the play-off series. You'll be surprised!"

CHAPTER 18

FOUR FOR FOUR

WILLIAM MALLOY was a happy man. Hadn't his Bears won two straight play-off games from the Mules and weren't the Parkville fans storming the gates and standing in lines which extended clear around Bear Stadium? And, to top it off, Eddie Duer had gotten by with Lefty Richards in the Tuesday game and with Windy Mills in the Wednesday game. That is, for eight innings.

Duer had called Kildane out of the bull pen to put out the fire when Mills got into trouble in the eighth. With the Bears leading 4 to 2 and one down, the Mules had loaded the bases on a single and two walks. But, true to form, Kildane had taken personal care of that little emergency by striking out Marreno and Fellows, and, in the bottom of the ninth, had set Conover, Roth, and Kinkaid down in order.

Malloy grinned at his manager and shoved the humidor across the desk. "Have a cigar, Eddie, and relax. You're ready to explode."

"Just about, boss," Duer agreed. "I'll be glad when *this* day is over."

"Scissors all right?"

"Right? Can't hold him! He even wanted to throw yesterday."

"Side bother him?"

"Says not, but you know him. Well, guess I'd better go down and suit up."

"Take it easy," Malloy protested, "it's only ten o'clock. You've got another hour. By the way, you changing the signs again today?"

"Nope, goin' with the same set."

Malloy was puzzled. "I'll never understand that. I still think Hilton was guessing."

Eddie Duer said nothing but, before he could control them, little laugh wrinkles appeared in the corners of his mouth. Malloy's sharp glance caught them and he gave Duer a long, suspicious look.

"You holding out on me, Eddie?"

"Well—er—I wouldn't say I was holding out, boss."

"But you know something about the signs I don't— that it?"

Duer nodded. "Yes, boss, I do! But I'd rather not tell you about it until the series is over."

"That means this afternoon," Malloy said pointedly. "All right, but just as soon as the game is over, I want you to give me all the dope. Right?"

"Right! And, boss—"

"Yes?"

"You're in for the shock of your life!"

Chip Hilton had enjoyed a series of shocks—all pleasant. He had been on tenterhooks Monday and right up to game time on Tuesday when every member of the

Hilton A.C. and half the neighborhood packed his mother's living room, hall, and porch to listen to the broadcast from Hedgetown. Chip had been thrilled by Corky Squill's great playing and by the Bears' 7–5 victory. But the 4–2 win on Wednesday had been the greatest surprise of all. No one would have believed that the Bears could take the Mules two in a row in view of the home-town club's great stretch-surge, but the Parkville heroes had done just that! Now . . . anything could happen.

Before Chip realized it, the game was on. For the Bears, it was Kildane and Curry. For the Mules, it was the do-or-die duo of Baker and Berry. And just as expected, the game developed into one of those tension-tight pitchers' duels were the breaks could mean victory or defeat.

The Bears drew first blood in the third. Hale drew a pass, Curry sacrificed him to second, and the hot-corner guardian slid safely into third on Kildane's fielder's choice. Then Corky Squill drove in the run with a sharp single to right and the Bears were out in front, 1 to 0.

That's the way it stood until the seventh when Kildane fogged a third-strike screwball low inside to Nick Marreno. The Mules' first sacker swung and the ball spun off Curry's glove. Before Mickey could recover the twisting speed ball, Marreno was on second, none away. Kildane then worked Fellows to the one-and-two count. But on an inside waste pitch, Fellows fell away and the ball hit his bat for one of those freak infield hits which no one can explain. At any rate, the ball went twisting and spinning down the third-base line and Fellows beat Hale's throw by an eyelash. That put Marreno on third and Conover's sacrifice squeeze bunt scored Marreno and advanced Fellows to second.

Then Roth broke Chip's heart and every other Bear fan's by connecting with an inside fast ball, sending the ball streaking down the hot-corner chalk line clear to the left-field fence. Fellows scored to make it 2 to 1 in favor of the Mules, and the tally held going into the last of the ninth.

There wasn't a sound in the room as Chip and his friends concentrated on the Bears' final time at bat. Hale walked and Curry's attempted sacrifice resulted in a pop fly to Berry, who fired the ball to first just missing the double play. That brought Kildane up to bat.

"Yes, folks, Duer is going to let Kildane hit— Can't understand that kind of baseball. Last of the ninth— behind two to one—a man on first and one down. I don't want to second-guess Eddie Duer, but in my book this calls for a pinch hitter—calls for Ketch Kerrigan—"

Soapy was shaking his head. "This is bad," he said sourly. "Kildane can't hit a lick."

"Quiet," Chip whispered. "He can bunt."

"—Kildane's not too good with the stick. The situation calls for a pinch hitter. Kildane will probably lay it down—I can't see this kind of strategy—"

"Scissors is taking his time getting up there. He's a big man, you know—six-six. He's had none for three today—bats from the third-base side of the plate—

"Baker sets—there's the stretch—here's the pitch— low and outside for ball one. They pitch 'em low and outside or high and inside to the big fellow. The Mules are playing in close—"

Just then Petey Jackson came charging up on the porch and elbowed his way into the sitting room. "What happened?" he exploded. "Who's win—"

"Shut up!"

"—around the knees and caught the outside corner to even the count. One and one now and Kildane steps

out of the box. He's looking down the line at manager
Eddie Duer in the third-base coaching box—this is an
important pitch—"

Chip's thoughts raced back to his last talk with the
tall chucker. Kildane had stressed the important part
that a knowledge of the opposing hitters' weaknesses
played in a pitcher's success. "They sure know mine,"
he had said wryly. "Why, I haven't looked at a ball near
the middle of the strike zone since I hit the league."

"—and it's low and outside—two and one now and
Kildane's ahead of Baker. There's bad blood between
these two chuckers—

"Baker stretches—lowers his hands—here's the pitch
—it's high and inside and it's too close. Kildane didn't
move a muscle—he's got guts—he wants on—listen to
this crowd—three and one now and Berry is calling
'time' and walking out to the mound and there goes
Gabby Breen. Breen might lift Baker—the big fellow's
got himself in a hole now for sure. Kildane's out of the
batter's box—he's looking at Duer—Squill's on deck—
in the circle—he's had three for three today—

"Folks, I can't understand Duer's strategy. He could
put Kerrigan in to bat for Kildane even now—lots of
fans are yelling for Ketch right now, but Duer's stick-
ing to his guns. I guess he's playing for the tie run—

"It's a cinch the Mules aren't going to let that winning run get on—not with Squill on deck—"

Chip couldn't understand any part of this game,
couldn't understand Corky Squill. What if he had been
wrong? It sure looked like it. Corky had hit three
straight times and had scored the only run for the
Bears.

"—Kildane's back in the batter's box now. He isn't
scared up there—the big fellow crowds the plate, you
know, and when he hinges those long arms and sticks

his elbows out over the dish—well, he's tough to throw to and that puts all the pressure on Baker. Skids might pass him—might hit him—too—and put the winning run on base—

"Gabby Breen sure doesn't want Baker to pass Kildane—not with Mister Poison on deck. No, he'll pitch to Scissors. Here comes Breen—he's going to ride it out with Baker—

"Kildane could win his own game and the pennant on this next pitch—if he could park one over the fence. He's got the power but every pitcher in the league knows his weakness for the high and the low pitches. The Mules are playing deep now—playing for the force —and the double play—

"Baker stretches—it's a tense moment—you can hear a pin drop here right now—here comes the pitch. Kildane's taking it—it's in there—right across the middle of the plate—it's a called strike for the full count. Hear that crowd—this is real baseball drama—and it's the first time I ever saw a chucker put one across the middle for the big guy."

Soapy couldn't stand the tension. He shuffled his feet and cleared his throat and managed a hoarse whisper. "Knock it outta the lot, Scissors, please."

"—and here it comes—it's a—"

"C-R-A-C-K!"

Chip heard the thunderous cheer almost as soon as he heard the crack of the bat, but that was all he could hear even though the announcer was shouting at the top of his voice. It seemed an hour before the words began to come through the speaker of the radio.

"—right on the nose and beat it out. I'll never know how Bates made that stop—the ball was far to his right, but he dove for it and made a backhand stop and held Curry at second. Bates might have caught Curry on the play if he hadn't been lying on the ground, because Mickey had made the turn and barely beat the throw back to the bag—

"Breen's out on the field now—the winning run is on and Breen doesn't like that. Time is out and the Mule dugout is riding Corky Squill now and Squill's talking back to them. This is a tense moment, folks, and you can understand the bench jockeying I'm sure. The whole Mule team and the fans and Gabby Breen and every player in the Mule dugout will be on Squill now—

"Breen's starting back to the dugout. He's yelling at Squill through cupped hands again and the Bear star is talking back. Here comes Eddie Duer. Duer's running toward Breen—looks like there's going to be trouble—they're nose to nose now. *There they go!* The players are running up—and here come the cops. They're swinging—Duer and Breen are swinging away at one another. Now the police are in there—they've got them separated. The rhubarb is all over—some fun!

"The umpires are taking charge now. No—wait a minute—hold everything. They're sending Breen and Duer to the showers. Yep. There they go—both of them—

"Bob Reiter is taking Duer's place in the third-base coaching box. Baker is ready to pitch. Squill is stepping into the box—bats righty, you know. Runners on first and second. Mickey Curry's on second with the tying run, and Scissors Kildane is on first with the winning run. Corky Squill's at bat—one of the best infielders in the business, you know—been in a bad slump for the past few weeks but he's sure out of it now. Came out of it in the Sunday game when the Bears had to win. Squill's had three for three so far in this game and he's up there now with a chance to win the game—

"Baker stretches—he's looking back at Curry on second. The Mules will be playing for the double play. Curry's taking a short lead off the keystone sack. Kildane is just a step away from first. Here's the pitch —it's outside—

"Baker stretches—he's looking back at Curry—seems nervous—it's a strike. Turner and Buster Lewis are throwing fast in the Mule bull pen. One and one—

"Squill steps back out of the box and Baker steps back off the hill. This is a tense moment. Corky's back in there now. Here comes the pitch—Squill swings— foul—Squill got a piece of it—it's back on the screen— one and two now. Baker's ahead of Squill now—won't give the little guy anything good."

Chip was completely in a fog, just couldn't understand it. But he knew one thing. He must have been wrong about Corky Squill. Why, it was even possible that he had been wrong about the whole thing.

"—that evens the count now and this suspense is almost unbearable. You can almost hear it crackle through this crowd. You can hear yourself think up here now— can hear the streetcars four or five blocks away.

"Baker stretches—lowers his arms—holds it there a second—here's the pitch.

"C-R-A-C-K!" The radio nearly leaped off of the table with the force of the cheer which swept out through the speaker. A fellow would have thought he was right in the ball park, under the grandstand. And the clamor and the continuous crowd-roar completely blanked out the announcer and every sound except the mad booming of thousands of voices in an unintelligible roar. For almost an eternity, it seemed to Chip, the speaker was dead except for the tremendous sound, and then, as it thinned out, the announcer, yelling at the top of his voice directly into the mike, began to make his voice heard. But Chip didn't hear the announcer, didn't know that Corky Squill had tripled against the right-field wall, and that Curry had scored, and that Scissors Kildane had slid almost from third base head-long with his long right arm stretched out like a fishing pole through and beyond Bingo Berry to score the winning run and clinch the pennant for the Bears.

Chip knew the Bears had won, knew it because of the roar of the Parkville fans, knew it in his heart because it was right. And while the announcer shouted, Chip was out on that field chasing Scissors toward the dugout and joining the Bears in lifting the happy chucker to their shoulders. Yes, Chip was one of those who pounded Corky Squill on the back and pulled his cap down over his eyes and then helped hoist Eddie Duer up in the air. . . .

And Chip saw the flare of the flash bulbs as the photographers took the pictures of the new champions of the Midwestern League and all the time he was thinking of the tragic mistake he had made with respect to Corky Squill.

"—a madhouse, ladies and gentlemen—absolutely a madhouse— These Parkville fans are insane. The crowd's down on the field now and they've got Eddie Duer and Scissors Kildane and Corky Squill up on top of the dugout and they're throwing hats and programs and shouting and yelling and cheering. And now they've got Bill Malloy—the owner of the Bears—"

Chip then realized that Soapy and Red and Biggie and Speed were pounding and punching him and he heard them for the first time.

"They did it, Chipper! They did it!"

"Let's celebrate!"

"Send them a telegram!"

"Boy, oh boy, that Corky Squill!"

"That Kildane!"

"Yeah, and that Eddie Duer!"

One would have thought Valley Falls had won that pennant, that Eddie Duer and Scissors Kildane and the Bears were local heroes. And, indeed, they were! To Chip Hilton and the members of the Hilton A.C.!

CHAPTER 19

ON TOP OF THE WORLD

THE PARKVILLE FANS wouldn't go home and there wasn't anything the stadium police could do about it. Bill Meadows and his crew of grounds keepers tried in vain to keep the frenzied rooters off the precious infield grass but were swept along with the crowd like leaves before an October breeze. Under the grandstand and in the clubhouse the joyous crowd was packed so tight that the Bears couldn't even get to their lockers. They were surrounded by frenzied fans who wanted to shake their hands or simply touch their uniforms. It took the Bears an hour to get themselves inside and the fans outside the dressing room. By that time they were dead tired. They sat in front of their lockers and relaxed for the first time in days.

"That play-off money is gonna get me a long rest and do I need it!"

"Me! I'm hittin' for the Rockies! Fish? They follow me right up to my cabin!"

"Boy, that crowd! I never saw anything like it!"

"They're gonna tear this town apart!"

"Scissors, you old goat, I could kiss ya! I think I will!"

197

"How about that Corky? Four for four and that last one— Hey, where is Corky?"

"I haven't seen him since he hit that ball!"

"Maybe he's locked out!"

"Naw, the door isn't locked."

"How about Eddie? Anyone seen Eddie?"

"Ain't seen him since he was chased!"

"Something screwy goin' on. Where's Malloy? We win the pennant an' those guys disappear."

"S'pose Corky's in trouble?"

"Naw, signing autographs more'n likely. Someone answer that crazy phone!"

They all had heard the persistent ringing but had ignored it. Finally Bob Reiter picked up the receiver.

"Hello, clubhouse. . . . Yeah, Eddie? . . . Sure! Everyone but Corky. . . . Oh, he is! Well, that's good. We were gettin' worried. . . . Yes, yes, I'm listening. . . . Okay, I've got it. Party at Sullivan's, Friday night, and there's a meeting at the hotel tomorrow afternoon. . . . Sure I'll tell them! See you in the morning!"

The players waited expectantly while Reiter cradled the receiver. The one-way conversation had excited their curiosity.

"What goes?" Curry demanded.

Reiter grinned. "Everything and anything," he drawled. "Malloy and Duer are tied up, but they said they knew you could do it, and they'd tell you personally tomorrow. Corky's with them in the office and there's a meeting at four o'clock tomorrow at the park, no one excused. And the party's at Sullivan's—eight o'clock tomorrow night. And, Scissors—they want to see you right away."

"That all?" Hale queried innocently.

"Something's goin' on," Klein said flatly. "You know what it is?"

"I just work here, my friend," Reiter said pointedly. "Why don't you ask them yourself? There's the phone."

They turned on Kildane, then, besieging him with questions. But he was as much in the dark as Reiter.

"Heck with it!" Curry grunted. "Why worry? We'll find out all about it tomorrow."

"Probably be in the papers!" Johnson quipped. "Me, I'm going to go get the biggest steak in town! S'long, Scissors, I'll wait for you at the hotel."

Johnson waited and so did about every other person in Parkville that evening. The Park Hotel was surrounded outside and jammed inside with fans who wanted to celebrate with the Bears in general and with Scissors Kildane and Corky Squill in particular. But they never showed up and didn't turn up until the next night.

Eddie Duer would say only that they had gone on a trip concerned with the banquet. The strange companions showed up at Sullivan's Friday night, all right, and they were accompanied by Chip Hilton.

Chip had hoped that Kildane would call him right after Thursday's game, but the call never came. He was disappointed but that was nothing compared to the shock he received early Friday morning. Chip and his mother had just finished breakfast when the doorbell pealed. In fact, the bell never stopped.

"Soapy!" Chip growled. "He'll wear that bell out."

The ringing continued until Chip opened the door. Kildane and Squill rushed in, then, and Chip could scarcely believe his eyes.

"Scissors! Corky!"

"Right!" the visitors chorused.

"What—what are you doing here?"

"We've come to get you!" Kildane said, pulling Chip

into the living room. "Come on, get your duds. You're goin' to Parkville with us and we're leaving in ten minutes. It's a long drive."

"Parkville? Why—"

"Parkville?" Mary Hilton echoed. "What for?"

"That's right," Kildane said. "You're Chip's mother, aren't you? Anyone would know that! This is Corky Squill, Mrs. Hilton, and I'm Scissors Kildane. Pardon us for being so abrupt, but Mr. Malloy, that's our boss, sent us out here to get Chip and bring him back alive for the pennant banquet."

"But—"

"No buts and no ifs! We're takin' Chip back with us. We'll take you, too, if you'll go! Those are Bill Malloy's orders."

"And orders is orders," Squill added. "Especially Malloy's!"

"But I can't," Chip protested. "I've got to leave Sunday for football camp."

"You can catch the train tomorrow night and you'll be back here early Sunday morning."

"But why? Why does Mr. Malloy want to see me?"

"What do you mean Malloy?" Kildane blustered. "How about the rest of us? Heck, we all want you to come. Don't we, Corky?"

Squill was emphatic. "We sure do! Me, particularly!"

Chip was confused, completely upset by the friendly spirit Kildane and Squill showed toward each other. Something had happened and he was completely in the dark. Again he was chilled by the thought that he had misjudged Corky Squill. And he was doubly bewildered by Squill's friendly attitude. What could have happened? And who had given Corky a black eye?

"Well, let's go," Kildane growled good-naturedly. "It's a long drive."

"Is it all right with you, Mrs. Hilton?" Squill asked.

"Why, yes," Mary Hilton said hesitantly, "if Chip wants to go—"

"All right, then," Kildane said happily, slapping Chip on the shoulder. "Let's go—or we'll never make it!"

They made it. A little tired and a little grimy, but on time. Chip was besieged by the happy ballplayers who were on top of the world. After the dessert had been served, Bill Malloy took charge.

"Men," the popular club owner began, "this little dinner is no accident. Eddie and I planned it a long time ago as well as several other surprises you are going to enjoy.

"At first we thought we'd make it big, invite the public at say ten dollars a plate. But we changed our minds toward the end of the race and I think you'll enjoy this family gathering just as much. After a little speechmakin', we'll adjourn to the Paradise Club where we've reserved all the floor tables. Eddie tells me they've got a big show planned and it's all in your honor.

"Now, for my little personal surprise. I have some checks here. The pennant bonus checks, your salary checks, and a special club reward check for every one of you. I think you'll like the figures."

Bill Malloy got the answer right then in a tremendous round of applause. You could tell Bill Malloy appreciated the response, but he held up his hands for silence.

"Now for the club surprise. Eddie Duer cooked this one up so he gets the credit. Of course Eddie was nice enough to arrange things so I could pick up the tab."

A burst of laughter greeted that statement. Every person in the room knew how well Eddie Duer could work money out of Bill Malloy.

"I'll assure you it didn't require much urging. Give me a hand here Eddie, Bob—"

Malloy picked up a small box and opened it. Everyone could see it was a ring and everyone could see there was a diamond set in the middle of the split baseball. It was a championship diamond ring just like those the big-league pennant winners received. The rafters rang with applause again, and, as each player made his way up to the head table for his checks and ring, every person in the place stood on his feet and cheered.

"Corky Squill, Bucky Boyd, Bill Dawson, Stretch Johnson, Norman Klein, Ted Smith, Paul Hale, Mickey Curry, and Scissors Kildane."

Yes, Malloy called the batting order first, with Scissors Kildane in the ninth spot. And then he called the rest. Kerrigan and Richards and Mills and Akers and Falls and Bob Reiter and, finally, Eddie Duer.

They nearly lifted the roof, then, giving the likable manager an ovation which brought tears to his eyes. But he stood there, unashamed and proud and happy until Malloy finally quieted the assembly and continued.

"That ends my part of the program. Eddie, you're on. Take over."

Eddie Duer needed time right then and the roar of appreciation the players accorded Malloy served the purpose. But Duer's voice was shaky and the words came slow and hard at first.

"Thanks—er—fellows for everything. I've already expressed my thanks to Mr. Malloy."

"It was the checks!" Malloy said dryly.

That brought a tremendous laugh and Duer was himself again when it quieted. He looked around and finally located the person he wanted.

"Now, I want to introduce Corky Squill. Corky has something to say and asked me if he might get it off his chest tonight. I know what he's going to talk about and

I'm sure you will remember it a long time. I guess I don't have to tell you that Corky Squill is, in my opinion, the best second sacker in the game."

Again the room rang with applause and cheers. And, if there was surprise in the hearts of some of those present, it wasn't evident in the tribute Squill received. Corky was embarrassed but determined, the same lead-off fighter who had played so brilliantly in the clutch games. He started right off, just as much to the point as was his custom in the games.

"Thanks, Mr. Duer. Fellows, I want to talk about the signs. All of you wondered what it was all about when the Mules began to get our signs. Well, I'm the guy that gave them away."

In the dead silence that followed Corky's statement, Chip held his breath.

"Yes, I gave the signs to the Bears. Not intentionally, but because I was a sorehead. Because I allowed myself to be bitter and jealous and small and the tool of an unscrupulous man—

"Yes, Gabby Breen manipulated me like a monkey on a string. Played on my ego and fed my jealousy and then used me unconsciously to betray my team.

"It's a long story and I won't bore you with the details, but Gabby Breen started me in baseball, coached me, and was my first manager. He got to know me so well that he realized that I gave the signs away by my motions and shiftin' of position in the field. So Breen changed my style, made me stand absolutely still after I got the signs. But he didn't tell me why— He didn't tell me anything but a pack of lies then—and later.

"I guess I was pretty cheap, but I got to grousin' because Eddie slapped a coupla fines on me and then Gabby happened along and egged me on. That was before he knew he was goin' to manage the Mules but it's no excuse. I shouldn't have fraternized with him because he was a member of another organization.

"When Gabby saw he was goin' to get the managin' job, he really went to work on me and fed me a lot of come-on lies about bein' the captain of the Mules next year and gettin' a big increase in salary and everything. Then he gave me a line about Hoot Kearns likin' his second baseman to be a hustler and he got me to change my style in the field right back to my old way of playin'.

"You know why, now. I fell for it. It was like takin' candy from a baby. Gabby said Kearns liked hustlin', jumpin'-jack, holler guys at second and as the team captain. You can see how stupid I was and am.

"I have another ring here that Mr. Malloy gave me. He said I could have the honor of presentin' it to the guy who got wise to Breen's trickery and to my stupidity. I asked for the privilege because I want to use the opportunity to apologize to him for a lot of ridin' and because I want you to know that he made it possible for us to win the pennant. This guy told me what I was doin', how I was givin' the signs away, and I promptly told Eddie. We never let on to anyone else, but I just crossed up Mr. Gabby Breen by usin' my same old motions and actions—but for the wrong pitches.

"Gabby didn't get wise until the final game and that's why I'm wearin' this little shiner. But that's another story and right now I want to give this ring to the swellest guy I ever met.

"Fellows, I'm referrin' to Chip Hilton!"

The roof fell in, then, deafening Chip and making it impossible for him to move. Now he could see the whole picture. Chip never knew how he got up to that table nor what he said nor what the Paradise floor show that followed was all about.

But Chip did know that he was wearing a championship baseball ring with a diamond in it and that he shared a table the rest of that evening with two of the finest friends he would ever have—Scissors Kildane and Corky Squill.

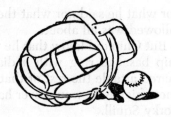

not what in ... or what the Paradise floor show that

followed ... about ...

that ... that he was wearing a champion-

ship ... the diamond in it and that he

sho ... the ... at evening with two of the

im ... ... have—Scissors Kildane and

Corky Squill.

CHAPTER 20

A TOKEN OF FRIENDSHIP

CHIP HILTON was the only quiet person in Speed Morris'
jalopy. Speed, Biggie Cohen, Red Schwartz, and Soapy
Smith were firing questions at him a mile a minute. Yes,
the gang had met him at the train and now they wanted
to talk about Scissors Kildane, Eddie Duer, Bill Malloy,
Stretch Johnson, and Corky Squill. The nearness of his
friends and the evident pleasure they derived from
hearing all about the banquet caused a surge of thank-
fulness to well up in Chip's heart. It was swell to have
friends like these, fellows you had grown up with and
teamed up with on the football field and on the diamond and on the court. And it was swell to make new
friends, too. His thoughts went speeding back to those
last few minutes on the platform in Parkville when he
was waiting for his train. Kildane had left him alone
with Squill for a few minutes and Chip had come to
know Corky Squill right then. Really know him. Even
now, Chip could hear the words the second sacker had
spoken, could hear them just as if Corky was saying
them all over again.

"You see, Chip, it's easy for some kids to fall under
the influence of men like Gabby Breen. Lots of kids

don't have good homes, fathers and mothers to guide them and help them with their problems. And not every boy has a chance to play on a school team and get good coachin' and have the advice of a good man.

"I went to school only as long as the law made me go and then I quit. I always wanted to be a ballplayer and Gabby Breen was the only person who ever paid any attention to me at all. Everyone else brushed me off and told me I'd been seein' too many movies."

Squill had grinned, then, and hitched up his trousers so the creases would hold. Then he continued. "I guess they were right. I always took in every sports movie I could and whenever a baseball game was broadcast or televised you could bet I'd be there. Then, one day, I was playin' in a sand-lot game and, after the game, one of the guys said a big-league scout was in the stands and wanted to see me.

"I thought the guy was kiddin' but he wasn't. Breen *did* want to see me and he took my name and address and then I didn't hear any more from him and I figured he'd forgotten me.

"But the next spring I got a letter to report at a little town in Ohio and I took my glove and spikes and hitchhiked a ride over there and tried out with about a hundred other kids. That night, Breen signed me to a contract.

"I was the happiest bozo in the world from that minute on and Gabby Breen was the Number One guy in my life.

"Then he got me in the Tri-State and then Wilkton and then Parkville—and, well, I guess I'd a jumped off the bridge if Gabby had said so. Right after you showed up for the All-Star game, Gabby asked me to contact you and I did. I figured I owed him any favor I could grant and it didn't seem like a very big one at the time, especially when he said I could make three thousand dollars if you signed up with him. I'm sure glad you didn't!"

Squill had paused, then, and Chip could see the bitterness in Corky's eyes. After a moment he had continued, choosing his words carefully.

"Gabby kept leadin' me on, and sellin' me a bill of goods about bein' field captain of the Mules and gettin' a big increase in salary and all that stuff. And that's why I went back to hustlin' the way I used to when I first started out. Only it wasn't hustlin', it was nervousness, mostly."

A little smile had played about the corners of Corky's mouth and he had chuckled wryly. "I fell for that like a ton of bricks. Of course I didn't know what Gabby had in mind and—well, you know the rest. Gabby knew I gave the signs away with my motions and shiftin' about and he figured he could call every pitch. Figured right, too! I realize it now, but I never gave it a thought until you talked to me that night. I was pretty sore at the time, Chip.

"But after I thought it through I knew you were right and I realized how close I had come to lettin' down the team and playin' right into Breen's hands. Anyway, I crossed him up in the next game and after we won the play-off I—but I'm gettin' ahead of my story.

"That Saturday night was the longest in my life. I thought about you and Breen and the team and the signs and how close I had come to losin' the pennant for all the guys and the people of Parkville and how close I had come to ruinin' my whole career and then on Sunday mornin'—

"Chip, I hadn't been to church for years. But I went that Sunday. That's why I missed the bus to the park and the reason Duer pinned another fine on me. But it was worth it, for it gave me the courage to go to Duer and tell him there would be no more sign stealin'. And at the banquet it gave me the courage to stand up in front of the gang and tell them just what had happened. The fellows were sure swell to me, Chip.

"Oh, yes. I don't know whether anyone told you what happened after the championship game. Anyway, Breen found me in the crowd and let me have one in the eye. That was bad news for him, for the police picked him up and rushed him up to Mr. Malloy's office and they sent for Mr. Kearns and I told them the whole story. I guess you saw that Breen had resigned, only that wasn't exactly right. Mr. Kearns fired him right there in Mr. Malloy's office.

"Chip, I don't know how I can thank you for bein' such a swell guy and havin' nerve enough to come to me that night and tell me exactly what was goin' on. I wish I knew—"

Corky had stopped then and Chip knew that the pivot star's emotions had caught up with him. But Chip hadn't been prepared for Corky's next move, hardly knew what had happened until later. But he could still hear the tremor in Corky's voice and feel the awkward hand-clasp.

"And—er—Chip, I wish you'd do me a favor. I wish you'd trade rings with me. I know our names are inscribed in them, but just wearin' your ring and lookin' at it once in a while will make me remember how close I came to makin' a terrible mistake and maybe it will save me a lot of trouble sometime. That is, if you won't mind wearin' *my* ring."

Squill's voice had trailed off but it hadn't mattered. Chip had slipped Corky's ring on his finger and had grasped the husky infielder's hand in a gesture of friendship and understanding. And the clasped hands erased

completely and forever all the ill feeling and rancor
which once had burned in their hearts.

How easy to misjudge a person . . . and how easy
to fall for a seemingly obvious fact. Why, he could have
ruined Corky Squill's reputation for life just because he
had believed the worst. Chip breathed a sigh of thank-
fulness. He was sure glad he had kept the details of his
discovery to himself.

And now, as Chip absent-mindedly turned the ring
on his finger, he lived to the fullest one of those never
to be forgotten moments which come to a fellow when
someone who has been regarded as an enemy suddenly
proves to be a friend and does something really big
. . . acknowledges a mistake and is gracious enough to
offer his most precious possession as a token of his
friendship.

At that moment Soapy's laughing voice cut through
Chip's thoughts and brought him back to the present.
Gosh, tonight he'd be leaving with the gang for State's
football camp and he'd be with the Rock again and
making new friends and starting out on his quest for a
college education. . . .

"How about that!" Soapy shouted. "How about that
Malloy saying he was gonna bring the whole team up to
our first frosh game? You think he will?"

Chip grinned in the dark. He wasn't too sure William
Malloy wouldn't do just that.

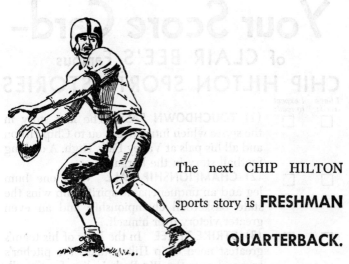

The next CHIP HILTON

sports story is **FRESHMAN**

QUARTERBACK.

Yes, young Chip is at State University at last, the same university where his dad had been a football hero in his time.

Don't miss this thrilling football story!

Your Score Card—
of CLAIR BEE'S Famous
CHIP HILTON SPORTS STORIES

I have read: *I expect to read:*

☐ ☐ **(1) TOUCHDOWN PASS** The first story in the series which introduces you to Chip Hilton and all his pals at Valley Falls High. A corking football story in the bargain.

☐ ☐ **(2) CHAMPIONSHIP BALL** With one bum leg and an unquenchable spirit Chip wins the state basketball championship and an even greater victory over himself.

☐ ☐ **(3) STRIKE THREE** In the hour of his team's greatest need Chip Hilton takes the pitcher's box and puts the Big Reds in line for the all-state honors.

☐ ☐ **(4) CLUTCH HITTER** Chip Hilton plays summer ball on the famous "Steeler" team and has a chance to use his head as well as his war-club.

☐ ☐ **(5) HOOP CRAZY** When the one-hand-shooting fever spreads to the Valley Falls basketball varsity, Chip Hilton has to do something, and do it fast!

☐ ☐ **(6) PITCHERS' DUEL** Valley Falls participates in the State Baseball Tournament and Chip Hilton pitches in a nineteen inning struggle that fans will long remember.

☐ ☐ **(7) A PASS AND A PRAYER** Chip's last football game for the Big Reds and how he kept the team together for his old coach.

☐ ☐ **(8) DUGOUT JINX** The story of the summer Chip spent with a professional team during its battle for the league pennant.

☐ ☐ **(9) FRESHMAN QUARTERBACK** This story finds Chip and some of his pals up at the State U. where the young star finds it tough to win a spot on the Frosh team.

Your local Bookseller has all of these books!